dexys midnight runners the team that dreams in caffs

Geoff Blythe / Mike Laye / Ian Snowball / Pete McKenna

First published 2014.

A Countdown Publishing paperback.

First published in Great Britain in 2013 by
Countdown Publishing Limited,
58 Bury Mead Road, Hitchin, Hertfordshire SG5 1RT.
www.countdownbooks.com

1st Edition.

ISBN 978-0-992 830434

A CIP catalogue record for this book
is available from the British Library.

Designed by
Hand Creative,
Suite B, 21A Bucklersbury, Hitchin, Hertfordshire SG5 1BG.
www.handcreative.com

Printed and bound in the UK by
Serendipity Print Limited
14 Sandringham, Brighton BN3 6XD.
Telephone: 01273 241417
www.serendipityprint.co.uk
james@serendipityprint.co.uk

This book is dedicated to the young soul rebels.

NO
WAY
OUT

HEDGES
Championships
NO
WAY
OUT

Searching For The Young Soul Rebels
Released July 1980

Kevin Rowland (singing), Kevin Archer (guitar/singing), Geoff 'JB' Blythe (saxophone), Big Jim Paterson (trombone), Steve Spooner (alto sax), Stoker (drums), Pete Williams (bass), Pete Saunders (organ), Andy Leek (organ on Geno and Thankfully Not Living In Yorkshire it Doesn't Apply).

Eight misfits walk into a room one day and come out with 'Searching For The Young Soul Rebels', an album which, to this day, is considered by many to be a classic and one of the most influential of its time.

This was a defining period in my life; I made some lifelong friends and what I learned and developed then has stayed with me to this day. I am proud to have been a part of it.

I have, here, related my personal experiences of this period to the best of my recollection, and hope I may be forgiven for any unintentional factual inaccuracies or omissions.

Lastly, it is my hope that others will get as much enjoyment from reading this book as I did in participating in its creation.

Geoff (JB) Blythe

This is not going to be a normal book about a group. It's not really about 'a group'. For a start, it covers such a short period. There is less than 12 months between the first and the last image. But, then, so there was between the release of the first home-grown single Dance Stance on Oddball Records in November 1979, through to the signing to EMI, the smash hit Geno of March 1980, the album Searching For The Young Soul Rebels in July 1980, to the car-smash breakup marked by the release of Keep It Part Two in October 1980. Less than twelve months.... So this clearly can't be the full story of that Dexys, who are still recording and performing today. What it is, though, is the story of another group, a group that, for many who were there, was, is and ever will be the only true Dexys. Dexys the band, not the brand. The team that met in caffs, that bade us Welcome to the New Soul Vision.

And then it isn't really *a book*, either. It's rather more like a film - a black-and- white one, clearly. A film that probably sits better now with the England of *Saturday Night and Sunday Morning*, the hand-held bravura of the French *nouvelle vague* or the celebration of everyday heroism in pre-fall Polish or Czech films. It's a film that seems to be a lot more of the 60's than of 1979/80, when it was actually shot.

This film is set in a landscape that looks like a foreign country to us now, from smoking on the Tube, to riding upstairs on municipal buses, to the derelict industrial wasteland that by now must be a Heritage Centre or a fashionable restaurant. For something else happened whilst Dexys were bunking the trains to London - Margaret Thatcher became Prime Minister on 4th May 1979. The background of these images is still that of a time before the seismic changes her government brought. A grey, monotonous cloud of a time that clung around the shoulders of the dying heavy industry, the stratified class structure, the bankrupt British Leyland producing dreadful cars, the three-day week, high inflation and a major oil crisis. No jobs, no hope, no future. The euphoric 1980s of rampant individualism, of privatisation, cappuccinos, footballers with Lamborghinis and 'Loadsa' Money' are still to come. When they vaulted the British Rail ticket barriers in the opening frame, this group literally hurled themselves out of Birmingham New Street and into a London narcissistically regarding itself in a New Romantic mirror. In almost all of these first scenes they are running, bursting from the streets north of Watford, restless in the streets of the capital and hungrily demanding that it should take note of them and their kind. This Dexys have been criticised for perverting Soul, for producing music with "no tenderness, no sex, no wit, no laughter" but, like the Northern Soul scene they referenced, they had simply appropriated it for their own purpose - to try to make some sense of a world that appeared to have no place in it for them. That's why they got such respect from their audiences, because they grabbed the embers of a punk that had finally been a betrayal, blew sax/Stax soul emotion on to them and produced a fierce burning flame that inspired and uplifted. And when you felt it, you could hook on to it straight away, with no outlandish haircuts and clothes that got you pointed at (or beaten up) in the street. Just a cheap workman's donkey jacket and a woolly hat would do it...

And then, finally, this is a film about betrayal. Dexys were a great band and Kevin Rowland was a genius of a front-man. He could play an audience like no-one else, except for maybe James Brown or a gospel-thumping Southern minister. He would force the hardest audience down into the absolute depth of toe-curling, arse-clenching, emotion-charged, embarrassed silence and then release them with a formidable blast of brass, organ, bass and drums. All the while making them bite on those home-truths baked in the lyrics. Together, this Dexys drove their crowd into a frenzy of excitement and passion, mirroring that Southern church in preaching the word, while delivering their congregation from everyday mundanity and irrelevance. Into something which, in this grey 70s Britain, very much resembled ecstasy. But the greatest magician fails as soon as he begins to mistake his own spells for reality and this team cracked like a glass Christmas ornament when they discovered that, legally and actually, they had now become just the hired hands. In this tragedy of Greek proportions, the front-man was left, literally, as the one-man band, who kept the name but lost the flame.

So, the last scene is Stoker, the power-house heartbeat of the band, still in donkey jacket and woolly hat, bag packed, alone and walking those darkened city streets once more. Here, as the final credits roll, is the real new romantic for those times, laid-off but resilient, on the road again and still searching for those young soul rebels.

Mike Laye

I didn't get into Dexys classic album, Searching For The Young Soul Rebels, from the off. The first time I heard Geno was around September/October 1980 and there was a good reason for that. For eight years I'd spent all my time, money, energy and passion on the northern soul scene in and around Blackpool and the legendary Wigan Casino Soul Club, host to the sweaty, jam packed, amphetamine fuelled, Saturday all-nighters that are still alive today in the memories of all the soulies who were regulars at Wigan back then, and what memories.

My mates and I threw ourselves into the northern scene hook, line and sinker, for better for worse, embracing all the good, bad and occasionally ugly aspects of the scene, as one does a marriage. I worked hard at it in order to keep it alive and together. There were times I absolutely loathed it and wanted to strangle it to death, in a manner of speaking. And there were other times we fucked each other senseless, bodies entwined, drained of all energy and emotion, sparked out on my bed watching the sun slowly rising, signalling the birth of a new day which meant I was one day closer to getting back to Wigan for another intravenous shot of northern soul, sweat, speed and priceless moments shared with like-minded people and so on and so on.

No doubt others did it differently to the way I did and all good and well to them for that but, for me and most of my mates in Blackpool, Preston and Burnley, the dawn of Sunday morning signalled the end of the good times and the beginning of another bleak, boring, five day landscape to get through, either working or unemployed. We lived like Shaolin monks, shunning almost everything connected to the reality of the outside world, including commercial music, apart from one or two notable exceptions. Like a prisoner locked up in his cell, northern soul was everything and anything else was complete and utter shite. Hours on end spent in solitary confinement, lying wasted on my bed and coming down from the effects of another all-nighter, listening to early Roxy and Bowie and my growing collection of imported stateside 45's. The impressive view of Blackpool Tower from my rattling, single glazed window, wearing my fingertips to the bone and learning every riff off of UB40's brilliant debut album, Signing Off.

Back to that cold windy September/ October night in Blackpool Mecca, not the Highland Room I must add, that was sadly long gone by then. There was me and my best mate, Ged, trying our best to adapt to normal life after almost eight years of soulful nocturnal isolation, back to the weekend rituals of dressing to the nines, swigging back beer and copping for girls I didn't really want, to waste time copping for aided and abetted by the odd sneaky black bomber or bluey to keep me bright eyed and bushy tailed, and the chat up lines flowing fast and furious. What was my name, what did I do for a living, what car did I drive, where did I like going on holiday and what was Wigan Casino all about? The same old fucking questions over and over again in order to play the mating game.

Although it still remained open for business, Wigan Casino and I were filing for divorce with no chance of a reconciliation. In our stormy, roller coaster relationship, we'd produced an offspring, northern soul and that was going to stay with me until I die. Many will, no doubt, disagree with me when I say that Wigan Casino was on its last legs. They will say that Wigan was still beating with its heart of soul stronger than ever but for me, the game we played between '74 and '77 was well and truly over, game, set and match to the inevitable passing of time and change. I wanted no part of the shenanigans involved in trying to sustain the memory of what would be talked about decades later as the greatest northern soul club, allegedly, that's ever been. Russ Winstanley, the man behind that wonderful legend, reminded me of Emperor Nero playing his fiddle, blind to everything happening around him while Rome was burning to the ground and that was both sad and unacceptable to me, who remembered the ambience, camaraderie and atmosphere of those early halcyon years.

I was bitterly disillusioned, lost and clueless, wondering where the last seven years of my life had gone while half-heartedly dancing with a girl to the Isley Brothers Tell Me It's Just A Rumour and as we were walking off the dance floor, I heard it for the first time. The horns in unison, the raucous chanting "Geno Geno Geno" blending oh so perfectly with the beautifully balanced brass section that kicked me in the bollocks in the nicest possible way.

A staccato attack of horns was marching around the dance floor, with me stood there thinking "what the fuck is this I'm listening too?" Fresh, bright, soulful and innovative music evoking many memories inside Wigan Casino, pulsing through me as the audience flocked to the floor, imitating a weird kind of hybrid skinhead, ska, skanking, stomping dance in time to the music and me wishing that I was back in '68 in a hot sweaty club watching Geno Washington.

I went out and bought the album the following Monday and began my relationship with Kevin Rowland's Dexys Midnight Runners, Searching For The Young Soul Rebels. Staring at the greenish glazed cover of the worried looking, black haired, street urchin carrying a suitcase and staring at the camera lens, frozen for all time. Who was he, where was he and where was he going? Studying the album lyrics night after night, trying to get to the bottom of this 'New Soul Vision' and what the songs meant. I went out and purchased a new Otto Link steel mouthpiece for my old, tarnished, tenor sax that gave me a much different sound, fuller and brighter to the old rubber one I used for playing along to UB40 with. Fuck going to work and all that bollocks because there was real work to do now, learning all the brass riffs, imagining I was one of the horn section standing shoulder to shoulder with Geoff Blythe and Big Jimmy in some cramped sweaty club, blowing my fucking brains out until my teeth ached and my lips swelled but fuck it, because I was a young soul rebel in search of the real truth, fuelling my dreams of one day making it as a sax player, playing quality soul music with a decent, tuned in band. My only problem being that I was never going to become a Midnight Runner but, sadly, by the release of their second album, Too-Rye-Ay, little remained of the 'New Soul Vision', which was responsible for captivating so many of us into Dexys and the whole idea they were trying to encapsulate back then.

For me personally, thirty three years after it was released, here I am still needing regular extra loud doses of the "New Soul Vision" to help keep me on the straight, narrow and optimistic side of life. Searching For The Young Soul Rebels still touches every fibre in me, as well as ticking all the boxes as to what makes a brilliant debut soul album. For many of us, soul music is all we have left after a long, boring, seemingly pointless week spent surviving in Boozebuster Britain, contributing to a crumbling society that is going tits up with no real solution in sight. A cold can and a relaxing bath on a Friday night. Smoke a joint or snort a line of Westminster approved charlie. Stick on Dexys nice and loud and soak away your aches, pains failed dreams and ambitions. Real quality soul music has the power to make you cry, laugh, regret, believe and convince you that tomorrow might just be your day. Kevin Rowland and Dexys Midnight Runners gave us all that in large doses, a free pass into the 'New Soul Vision', keeping the flame burning in us all who are still into the album, no matter how strong the wind blows and the rain pours because there is nothing like Searching For The Young Soul Rebels. One of the greatest UK soul albums ever to be etched in vinyl. Enough said.

Pete McKenna

Is Searching For the Young Soul Rebels the greatest debut album by a British band? In 2006 the NME voted it number 16 in the 100 Best British Albums Ever. What cannot be denied is that the album delivers a diverse mixture of songs that touch upon so many different influences. But perhaps what was is of more importance is the emotion compressed into each track. The songs, the album couldn't be compared to anything else at the time of its release and that remains the same over thirty years later. Often referred to in short cut; 'Rebels' to some, 'Searching' to others, which perhaps reflects something about that individual. For me both have applied but nowadays I align myself to 'Rebels' (I had a rebel then and I have a rebel spirit now - thankfully!). When the album came out I wasn't yet a teenager. I had yet to sample/dip my toe into/dive into what a 1980's teenage existence had to offer. By the time I had acquired 'Rebels' there had only been weeks between it and what would become the next most significant album in my life, Sound Affects. Then there was my two most important singles; That's Entertainment and Geno. Both were never far from my record player, and both were played to death in the youth club disco and juke box that I frequented.

Geno was the first song that I learnt to dance to. Well, it was a kind of a dance. It didn't involve too much thinking. All I was required to do was stand on the spot and take turns alternating raising one leg and kicking out - as if kicking an imaginary ball, then repeat the move with the other leg. The arms swung in a relaxed manner from side to the side and my head stayed in one spot, with eyes straight forward. Where I lived everyone did this dance.

I can picture myself now (over thirty years later), a vivid image of me dancing to Geno in the Maidstone Prison Officers and Postal Workers Civil Service Club. I (along with my sister and brother) was dragged there by my mum and dad on a regular basis, given a Tizer and a bag of salt and shake and left to our own devices while the adults did their thing. There were regular discos too and on one of these nights I saw something that would change my life. There was an older boy dancing to Geno, nothing unusual there, but what impressed me most was what he was wearing; a red V-neck jumper, white button down shirt, thin black tie, blue jeans and desert boots. It was my first introduction to fashion. There was something about him; his look, the way he danced. I did some research (possibly via my older sister) and learned that he was a mod. A few weeks later I returned to the Civil Service Club for another disco, only this time I was dressed exactly the same as that boy (fortunately he wasn't there and I never saw him again). All these years later I still regard that combination of red jumper and white button down shirt with high regard. So now I had Geno in my life, a look and I could dance. Being so young a matter of months seemed to last forever and, by the end of that year, I had begun my own personal voyage of discovery into music, fashion and dancing.

That summer I also acquired my own copy of the 'Rebels' album. Again, I have vivid recollections of that day. I was out in town with my new 'mod' mate, Neil. We were only young but Neil had an older brother called Paul. Somehow we merged with a larger collection of older mods, maybe twenty or so parka clad, Jam shoe wearing, teenagers. At some point Paul disappeared into Woolworths. Neil and I waited until Paul returned, grabbed us and hastily led us away to the Wander Inn café (where the mods hung out). We sat down at one of the tables and Paul emptied his Parka's deep pockets and placed several cassettes onto the table. There was a mixture of tapes, from bands like Bad Manners and The Beat, and amongst them were several copies of Searching For the Young Soul Rebels. Paul offered me one and I became a very proud (if not slightly paranoid) owner of my first Dexys album. The vinyl copy followed and both got played to death.
The 'Rebels' album became an important feature in my daily life as I discovered more about what mod was all about, and the music and clothes they liked. It was a great time and Rowland's words imprinted themselves onto me. I heard the calling, I wanted to be one of the soul rebels that he was talking about - I was one of them soul rebels!

Those words from Rowland are possibly the most evocative words I have ever heard in a song, they arrived at a point in the album where the climax is swelling, the end of a wonderful journey through ten previous songs, the soul vision welcomed and I embraced it whole heartedly, suspended in the arms of a lyrical genius, hanging in a moment of brilliance. Yes, I heard the calling to join the ranks of the soul rebels, soul brothers and sisters, and be part of the new soul vision - I still do!

Being part of this book is a privilege for me. It's another part, an extension of that soul rebels journey that began, for me, at that Civil Service Club in 1980. Just like the album still thrills, inspires and excites me, so was the process of putting this book together with Geoff, Mike and Pete, a collaboration I'm very grateful for! Searching For the Young Soul Rebels will be, for always, an album that has a special place in many people's hearts and souls. It is certainly one of the most revered albums of all time and will always be unique and important. This book is now a part of that story and yes, it is possibly the greatest debut British album of all time.

Ian Snowball

Enjoy
Coca-Cola
ONER
TAKE AWAY
BAB
CLASSIC
HOTEL
EATING
Classic Hotel
Kebab Take Away
4
MECCA
BOOKMAKERS

Euston

Euston

Euston

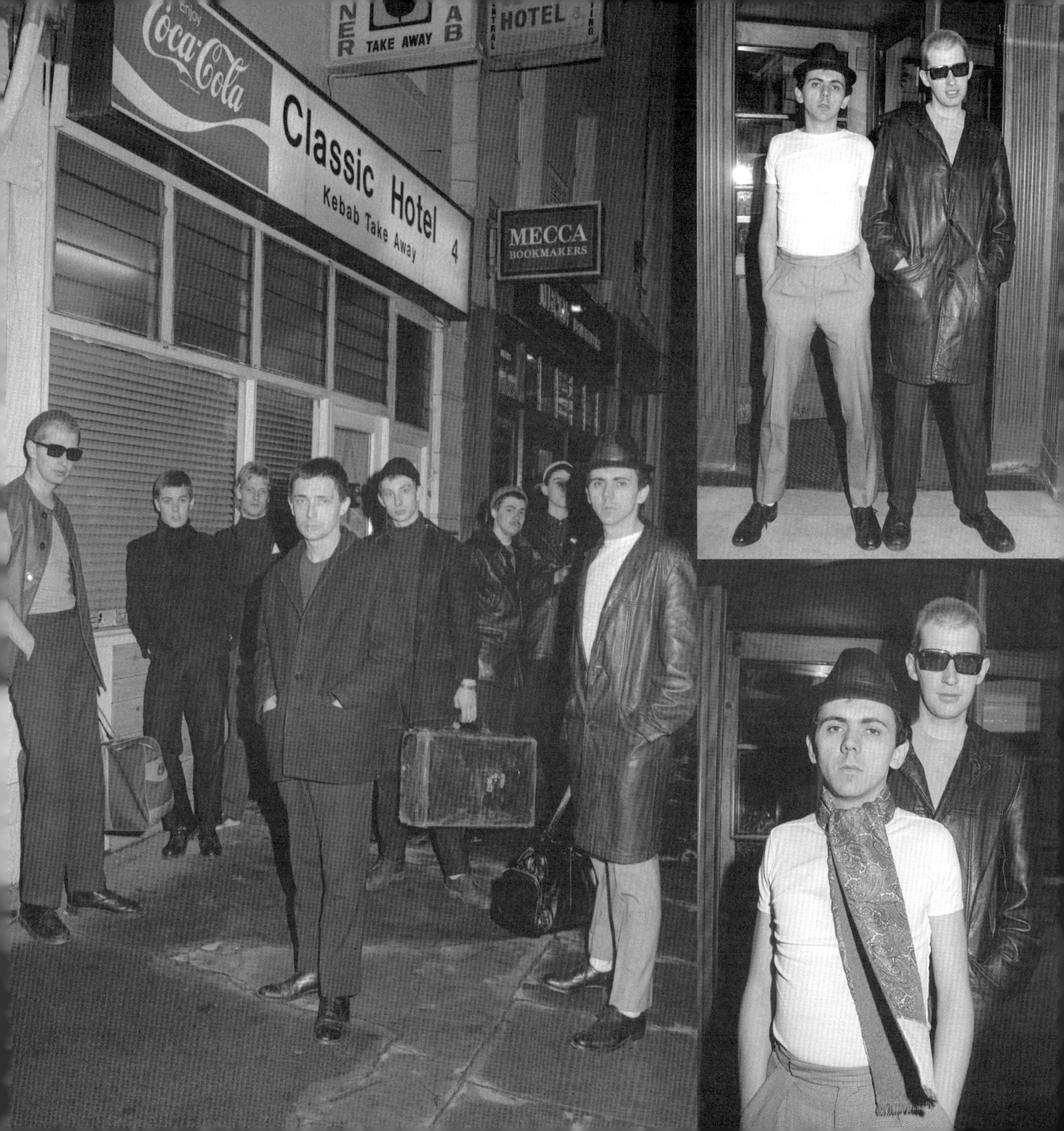
Enjoy
Coca-Cola
Classic Hotel
Kebab Take Away
4
TAKE AWAY
HOTEL
MECCA
BOOKMAKERS

PLATFORM 5 SOUTHBOUND
EUSTON
EUSTON
ROBERT COHEN

WAY OUT →
EUSTON
EUSTON
Craft in Action

by Bus
SCOTLAND THE BRAVE
ARGENTINA 78

COMBO 115
ROGERS

421
OPEN
LA CANTINA
HAMBURGERS

dexys
midnight
runners
the
team
that
dreams
in
caffs

From the get go, it was made crystal clear to all the members of Dexys Midnight Runners that there was only going to be one boss and that was Kevin Rowland, the general in charge of his foot soldiers, who had no choice but to do things his way or hit the highway. Egotistical, selfish, arrogant, determined and driven to achieve what he perceived to be pure, moving, musical excellence, Rowland was all these things and more. To most people unforgivable character traits but, surely, honourable members of the jury, in Rowland defence, he can be forgiven all of these faults when we consider the final product, born out of what many would perceive to be megalomania.

Hidden away from the publics' peeping eye after months of enduring a strict regime of exhausting keep fit sessions, with hours of rehearsals aimed at turning Dexys Midnight Runners into a band so visually and musically unique to anything that had gone before, Rowland unleashed the first part of his ultimate dream of The New Soul Vision on the unaware British youth in the form of the album, Searching For The Young Soul Rebels, on the 11th July 1980, comprising the following tracks in order of appearance: Burn It Down, Tell Me When My Light Turns Green, The Teams That Meet In Caffs, I'm Just Looking, Geno, 7 Days Is Too Long, I Couldn't Help It If I Tried, Thankfully Not Living In Yorkshire It Doesn't Apply, Keep It, Love Part One and There There My Dear.

The band members included Kev 'Al' Archer - guitar, Big Jimmy Paterson - trombone, Pete Williams - bass, Geoff Blythe - tenor sax, Steve 'Babyface' Spooner - alto sax, Pete Saunders - organ, Andy 'Stoker' Growcott - drums and Andy Leek - organ. Produced by the legendary Pete Wingfield, the album only lasts some forty one minutes and thirty seven seconds in total. Certainly not the longest album ever recorded but, then again, it's one of those rare albums that doesn't have to be long and drawn out to get its message across. The content of the album is soul music, combining traditional and gospel roots with northern soul with a twist, played by musicians who knew more than a thing or two about soul music and just what it's all about to those of us who are into such music. The album takes us on an emotional journey from start to finish, with songs reminiscent of situations which, for better or for worse, many of us have found ourselves in at some point in our lives, when all we've got is soul music and the dreams of better days to come.

A priceless collection of songs and instrumentals fuelled by a riotous cacophony of blistering horn riffs, driving beats, Hammond organs and stripped to the bone lyrics. Searching For The Young Soul Rebels is timeless music, one of the greatest debut albums which many bands only dream of recording, as fresh and as vibrant today as it was back then when it hit the charts 35 years ago. A time when we were all considerably younger than we are now, many at an age we never thought we'd even come close to reaching. A time when all of our hopes, dreams and ambitions were intact, when the impossible was easy and life was an everyday adventure. Like a master chef, Rowland served up mouth-watering cuisine which was devoid of unnecessary appetisers and that left us all craving for more of his New Soul Vision which is, of course, the essential hallmark of every delicious meal.

Dashing home from the record basement of Binns department store in Blackpool (before the building was destroyed by fire and renamed Boots) clutching the album, desperate to listen to everything the slab of vinyl contained, other than the chart topping, romping, stomping Geno, that took so many of us by surprise. None of us expecting to hear the album seconds after carefully dropping the needle on to the turntable, turning up the volume full blast - and fuck the neighbours - and kicked back to soak in what Kevin Rowland was offering.

burn it down

Searching For The Young Soul Rebels kicks off how it means to go on with the opening track, Burn It Down, with surely one of the most original and distinctive introductions to a song ever recorded. The sound of a transistor radio switched on high frequency, tuning various sounds from channel to channel searching for the right one. Muffled voices, marching music, Deep Purples Smoke On The Water, Sex Pistols No I Got No Reason Cause I'm Still Waiting, a quick shot of classical music followed by the Specials Working For The Rat Race, You're No Friend Of Mine. Sitting there wondering what the fuck was going on and what's all this nonsense got to do with what the critics labelled a truly great soul album, about to give up the ghost and consign it to the bottom of the LP pile as a bad buy never to be played again, ending all dreams and expectations in a couple of weird seconds forced to wait until the next so called contender to the throne comes along. The radio is turned off as Rowland's call to arms kicks in shouting to his troops, who resoundingly answer his call as one. "Big Jimmy? Yeah. Now. Yeah - For Gods Sakes Burn It Down". The song kicks off with a brilliant opening brass section riff that chills you to the bone and makes the hairs on the back of your neck stand to attention as the whole of the band jump in head first, building up a solid, stomping, soulful march, accompanied by Rowland's angry vocals that turn it into a protest statement for the Irish people.

With the 'troubles' becoming increasingly violent back then, Britain wasn't exactly the best place for a common or garden Irish wanderer to live. For many years the Irish people had served as the inspiration for British humour and ridicule and for Rowland, enough was enough. Burn It Down is his metaphorical sledgehammer he uses to smash the verbal abuse to bits. A noble but futile effort but, then again, if you don't try you don't get. As the song carries us through to the chorus, Rowland reels off an impressive list of names, some of the Emerald Isles greatest and respected writers and poets who through their talent for words have managed to stand the test of time. One cannot help thinking that Burn It Down is a cry to the heavens to recognise and treat the ordinary Irish people with respect. People like Oscar Wilde and George Bernard Shaw proving to the world that Ireland has so much more to offer than Leprechauns, potatoes and Guinness as Rowland spits out the lyrics "Shut you're fucking mouth till you know the truth" followed by a punchy brass crescendo slowly fading to silence, leaving us stunned and hungry for more of his New Soul Vision.

tell me when my light turns green

As Burn It Down fades to silence, leaving us stunned at what we've just heard and what can possibly follow to come near it. Moments later we're in for another pleasant shock as Tell Me When My Light Turns Green kicks in. A song similar in style and tempo to Burn It Down, supported from beginning to end by a heavy downpour of tight horn section riffs, fluctuating in various degrees of intensity as the pace rolls along at a solid pace until we're given a brief respite courtesy of Big Jim Paterson, who delivers one of the sweetest sounding trombone solos of all time that has become forever synonymous with the unique Dexys soul sound from the second the instruments mouthpiece touched his lips.

Essentially the song is a cry for help as a result of us hitting rock bottom, finding we've got nowhere to go and nobody to turn to in our hour of need. How many of us can admit we've been there at some point in our lives, that we've sincerely uttered the same words after life knocks us down when we least expect. Boozing, gambling, women and drugs, they're all out there waiting for us to take a bite, enticing us wander off the straight and narrow into a world of pain, tears and desperation until we have no choice but to turn to the almighty - those of us who believe in such a thing - and beg for help and absolution.

A hard hitting street level plea from the writer of the song who has himself been there many times over the course of his roller coaster musical career. Seen it all in his twenty three years, manically depressed and shedding tears as the angelic sound of the horns offer inspiration and a second chance to get back on his feet. Surely providing that we all adhere to the all-important social code of "treating others as we'd like to be treated", isn't it the right of fellow human beings who have fallen into the abyss to be given a second chance? Isn't that what life's all about?

the teams that meet in caffs

The Teams That Meet In Caffs is an instrumental track and what a cool piece of music it is, with the title providing the inspiration for the title of this book as well giving us some time out to relax from the blinding, stomping pace of Burn It Down and Tell Me When My Light Turns Green and enjoy the musicianship of Rowland's soldiers. With a sweet sounding, slightly jazzy, Kenny Jordan style guitar intro to ease us into the track, the brass section slowly kicks in with the organ providing a quirky background accompaniment before another staccato horn section attack, adding a sense of drama to the music almost as if we're sitting in a cinema listening to the title track of the big feature. Bass, drum, guitar, organ and horns all working together as one as the tempo and rhythm speed up, switching up from first to fifth gear followed by a four part marching style horn section riff before surrendering to a totally unexpected, but nevertheless welcome, wild, withering, moody saxophone solo courtesy of Geoff Blythe that now takes musical precedent, echoing ghostlike over the horns that continue relentlessly onwards, with their tight awesome sound complementing the sax perfectly as the music gradually fades to silence and we wait for the next slice of what is rapidly turning into a truly delicious, mouth-watering pie.

UK Café Culture really exploded after the end of the Second World War in many various guises, from the rough and ready, cheap and cheerful greasy spoon offering a brew and a full English fry up to interior designed outlets offering healthier menus to their discerning clients. Cafes have always been, and continue to be, many things to different people. Places where couples first met and fell in love. Where pensioners meet to warm up their cold bones on mugs of tea and, for many old people, the only point of contact they have with other people in their lonely lives. For the unemployed they offer a place to meet up and kill time to talk about their hopes, dreams and fears, trying to get a foot on the first rung of life's ladder. Even a few bands have been born out of the café culture, Dexys Midnight Runnners being one of them. There are cafes that serve as the headquarters for all types of teenagers, each into their own scenes. Hippies, ravers, goths, skinheads, bikers and mods and for the cool trendy fashion conscious London mods about town. There really is only one café to be seen in, where you can rub shoulders with musicians, artists and writers on any given day of the week. The Bar Italia on Frith Street Soho, home to Bohemia for centuries and the spiritual social home to mods stretching back to the days of swinging 60's London. It was first opened by an Italian couple called Lou and Caterina Polledri back in 1949 and quickly established itself as a hangout for Soho's Italian community, as well as acquiring the reputation many still regard today as serving up the best coffee in London.

In a constantly changing, often unacceptable world, so much of the Bar Italia's charm and popularity is down to the fact that it's resisted the kind of trendy change other cafes have fallen victim too. The original Gaggia coffee machine first installed over fifty years ago is still going stronger than ever today, hissing out creamy hot cappuccinos for the ever loyal clientele. And one can only imagine how many hundreds and thousands of feet have walked through the door, standing on the original floor carefully laid by the families Uncle before it opened for business. A true testament to the quality of traditional craftsmanship of a bygone time. Next time you're having a stroll around Soho, do yourself a favour and call in for a drink and a bite to eat. You won't be disappointed and you never know who you might be rubbing shoulders with.

i'm just looking

Rowland slows the pace right down with I'm Just Looking, as the track kicks off with his whispered lyrics accompanied by the organ that adds a distinctive gospel, church like quality throughout the track, broken up by yet another sequence of tight as a drum horn section riffs that are starting to typify the unique soul sound of Dexys at work. This time it's the turn of the small town music promoter/nightclub owner/ band manager who comes under Rowland's scathing attack. Egotistical wankers out for their own gains at the price of others. Penthouse provincial celebrities in their own minds, holed up in their own dreams and ambitions trying to win the game unaware that they've already lost before it begun.

Every town used to have one back in the day. Budding Peter Stringfellows' mixed in with a bit of Tony Wilson, who fancied dabbling in the local music scene purely because they saw an opportunity to become cool and trendy by hanging out and being seen with all the up and coming musicians, and their adoring sexy groupies who slavishly followed them around doting on their every move. On the surface these pseudo music entrepreneurs appeared to be good at what they did, championing the best of the bands on the local scene. Earnest promises to become their manager after a few free beers and chopping out lines in the bogs, to help establish the confidence and friendship between the parties.

After a successful debut gig, the town is buzzing as more gigs follow and attract the interests of various music journalists all eager to do a photo feature on the next big thing, in between studio rehearsals and recording sessions, all thanks to the managers' best mate. The owner of the antiquated studio who willingly agrees to give the lads some free time getting their act together before accepting a very generous, half price deal to cut a four track demo CD featuring their best tracks so their manager can spread the word among the bigger record companies in London, in the hope that he can secure a once in a life time recording contract that never materialises, leaving the boxes of demo discs gathering dust in the managers stockroom as he chops out another line. But hey, it's only rock and roll.

geno

Every debut album of any credible worth needs one track packed with chart potential and Geno, which is dedicated to the legendary soul artist Geno Washington, did it for Dexys Midnight Runners, storming into the number one spot in 1980 and thereby introducing to the masses the music of Kevin Rowland. In a world surrounded by big chart names and music, Geno was just so fresh, different and exciting and yet, somehow familiar to those of us tuned into such music, almost like bumping into an old friend you hadn't seen for years. From the powerful opening marching staccato horn section laying down the distinctive riff that quickly became popular in pubs and club sounding like a thousand car horns all going off at the same time. Seconds later the music is backed up by loud chanting "Geno, Geno, Geno, Geno" in unison, as the whole thing slowly blends into a soulful world of brass riffs, saxophones, trumpets and trombone all blowing as one, as the sound entices you into the hot, sweaty club you've been queuing up for ages to get in, hoping to be one of the lucky ones there to watch one of your soul heroes and inspirations in the form of the legendary Geno Washington.

Geno was a former American serviceman who liked the UK so much he decided to make a new life here once he'd completed his military service and began making a respectable name for himself as a great soul artist, backed up by his Ram Jam band. He was booked into the Clifton Bar Blackpool back in the mid-80's, a woefully ill advertised gig during which no more than seventeen people turned up to watch him. Not being the kind of performer to be put off by such a pitiful turn out, Geno took to the stage with his full piece horn section and, from the opening song, he turned up the heat and kept things red hot for over two and a half hours. What a night it turned out to be, with more than enough space on the dance floor to shuffle about in.

By the time the vocals kick in, short and sweet, weaving in and around the horn section riffs, you feel like you're in the club wearing your baggies and all leather dancing shoes. The one big night advertised for weeks, that's been keeping you going body and soul, playing truant from school and steering clear of fights and scrapes with the law or at least until you've seen Geno live that is. The first of the choruses blasts off, the horn section firing on all cylinders, bass guitar and the drum joining in, pounding out the spine tingling beat, ending in a crescendo of short, stabbing riffs before sliding effortlessly back into intro riffs that caught your full attention from the get go.

The mood in the club changes dramatically as Geno takes to the stage to begin a blistering set. He's your gear, your bombers, your Dexys, your high. You don't want any advice from anyone about where you're going wrong in school and life because you've got plenty of time for all that bollocks. You've got youth on your side, all your dreams and ambitions to go for and tonight. All Geno's job is to entertain you and inspire you to dance like never before. You're one of the hot, sweaty crowd standing there hailing and chanting his name from the top of your voice, shouting to the top. "Oh oh oh Geno". And for one mad, crazy moment a thought flashes into your mind. You think you could be as good as Geno one day. Get a band together, sweat soul, blood and tears for months until you get the sound you're searching for just right and, as the show comes to an emotional end, both you and Geno have gained something from the night. He fed you, bred you and you'll remember his name but can you do the same? "Oh oh Geno". The track fades to an end, the horns go silent and you're left standing there breathless, begging for more.

seven days too long

"Seven Days Is Too Long Without You Baby, Come On Back To Me". The words that form the chorus of a storming classic original northern soul track of the same name, recorded by Chuck Wood and released in 1967 on the BIG T record label. A track played in the Golden Torch, Twisted Wheel and Wigan Casino, not to mention the countless other clubs up and down the country that have helped to keep the northern soul flame burning bright and strong over the decades, keeping it firmly established as Britain's oldest surviving dance scene and a worthy track of music, which Dexys Midnight Runners pay justifiable homage to in their brilliant cover version.

The Dexys totally credible cover is virtually indistinguishable from the original single. The storming hundred miles an hour intro is all there note for note, leading up to the vocal introduction and the start of the song. It's only when the distinctive tone of Rowland's voice kicks in that you realise you are listening to a great cover version of a song loved by so many soulies out there, then and now, and Rowland's manages to do the subject of the song true justice which can only come from somebody who is truly into and loves all aspects of soul music because if you weren't such an undertaking would be impossible for fear of the backlash from critics and fans alike.

The subject matter of the song deals with the time honoured themes of love, relationships and breaking up, over what in reality is a stupid quarrel. Wanting to put the situation right and getting back together because, as we all know, during and after being in similar situations, there's nothing quite like breaking up and getting back together to put the love and passion back into a fading partnership. A magical time when you meet the person you fall head over heels in love with, thinking that they are the one you want to share your love and life with forever and a day. Blissfully happy in everything you do, together as one, unable to contemplate the thought of ever being apart like all couples do, lost in the early throes of love, sex and romance.

You know every curve, crevice and orifice of each other's body by the time love starts to slowly fade away and familiarity breeds contempt. The frequent rows that were once unthinkable become the norm and Friday nights out on the town with your respective mates, moaning and groaning about how bad things have got between you compared to how they used to be. That magical time you desperately want back as you reluctantly agree to sometime apart, a temporary split to give each other space and time to sort your heads out while deciding if you really do want to stay together or not.

A week apart is enough to get on the phone to arrange to meet up for a chat in a bid to clear the decks and start again but things have moved on beyond your control. You don't really want to break up but you don't want to fight for the love you once took for granted. The danger signs are written on both your faces, clear as day, as the reality kicks in. Sleepless nights taking their toll on you both, unable to concentrate and no time left to hang around for a reconciliation that might never happen. Telephone lies and excuses to each other that you want to be left alone, that started with a stupid lovers quarrel and has escalated into a spiteful, destructive force leaving one of you desperate to make up and get back together while the other still needs space and time to think because seven days is too long without you baby.

The one noticeable difference featured in Dexys version as opposed to the original that still manages to work well occurs towards the end of the song, in the form of a rousing hand clapping chorus of "7 Days Is Too Long Without You Baby" followed by a staccato brass attack, all blending together perfectly before the gradual fade to silence. All complements and respect to Dexys Midnight Runners for having pulled off a memorable version of the immortal Chuck Woods, fifty four year old northern soul floor filler.

i couldn't help it if i tried

A slow heavenly chorus of horns lull us into a false sense of security as Rowland's delivers another song about love and relationships, when two former lovers who once had it all going on gradually lose the love they shared through a mutual lack of interest in each other's bodies and minds, coupled with an inability to nurture and maintain a relationship that once promised so much love and happiness and is now dead on its feet.

A trade off, when one gives their heart in exchange for time, drinking each other's blood to the point where there's no more to drink and give. We've all journeyed down that innocent, happy, rose strewn path at some point; new love, holding hands, hearts skipping in a magical world far removed from the nitty-gritty of reality and day to day life, where dreams amount to nothing. Withering and dying as a new dawn rises, signalling the beginning of another hopeless, cold, bleak Monday morning in bed-sit land, begging the answer to the question "Where is the love gone we once shared and enjoyed and can we be arsed making the effort to get it back?"

Bodies once entwined together as one, caught up in the push and shove of passion, soaked in each other's sweat, saliva and semen and thinking that their rosy, romantic world will never end. That neither of them will eventually turn into emotionless icebergs, hopelessly drifting on a freezing cold sea of indifference. Two people barely going through the motions, in a futile attempt to not hurt each other's feelings, until the time comes when packing your bags and fucking off is the only dignified move to make. If only to pay respect to the death of an old love once strong, vibrant, colourful and alive that offered everything imaginable, leaving only regrets and tears as the door slams shut.

thankfully not living in yorkshire it doesn't apply

Thankfully Not Living In Yorkshire It Doesn't Apply has the quirkiest title of any song on the album but it's also the quirkiest musically. With its frenetic, relentless pace, Rowland's curious falsetto vocals and the songs "Ooh ooh ahh ahh" it combines a weird fusion of northern soul meets Doo-Wop that, on paper, is as opposite a concept as chalk and cheese but in Rowland's work, the song works well.

Based on experiences during time spent in Yorkshire, the song is a cutting piss take of a certain kind of narrow minded, egotistical, bigoted blokes who are found in large numbers in some areas and who are proud of it. Blokes fiercely proud of their origins, being born in the county they loving refer to as "Gods Country" and any person who happens to be born outside of their paradise are called "namby pamby's". Diehard jobsworths who live their lives the way their parents and grandparents did. "Get thee sen a job, get thee sen a decent woman and have a few kids. Graft ya bollocks off five days a week and more if necessary, week in week out and no going on the dole. And come the weekend lad, get thee sen down the working men's club with the lads, enjoying a skin full of bitter, entertained by a bunch of piss poor untalented cabaret artists who couldn't cut the mustard working in a zoo". It's a song like no other.

keep it

"Try and keep it safe, keep it cosy but it feels so out of place. You're feeling a loss but you're not fit to make it. You're offered so much but you're frightened to take it. Spout your lines, read all your books, you hear the sounds, miss all the hooks. Your best is what you least understand. You hate the graft, won't join the race. You're scared to scar your pretty face. Safe now cos your heads in the sand". Real cutting words penned by Dexys tenor sax man, Geoff Blythe, providing a fresh break from Rowland's distinctive rhetoric as the song begins with yet another trademark, soulful Dexys horn section riff and builds into a slow but solid rhythm, providing the introduction to a song taking the piss out of people who fail to put their money where their mouth is and step out of the front door of their safe, comfortable, narrow minded, Marks and Spencer existence just once in their lives.

Based on personal experience, Geoff sums up the kind of people we've all come across at some point during our lives. We all know the type, obsessive pseudo intellectuals who live their lives twenty four seven by the kind of books they read within the cosy confines of their wardrobe existence, without dipping their toes into the reality, sadness, cruelty, joy and pain the real world is full of. Reading and spouting about the misconceptions of a Bohemia lifestyle, struggling to survive from day to day in the big bad world is one thing but doing it is a completely different reality. Back in a previous life we used to have this favourite town centre pub called the Criterion in Blackpool. It was a rough and ready, spit and sawdust affair without a jukebox but what it did have was atmosphere rarely found in other pubs.

Packed to rafters every weekend with all kinds of people, young and old, from all backgrounds, from cherry red skinheads out for a few beers after another Saturday afternoon terrace war, to pissed up tired old pensioners and university students. A few of them coming from comfortable backgrounds that allowed them to gorge themselves on Kerouac, Proust, Marx, Engels, Lenin and Camus. Listening to them ranting on about how they were going to become great philosophers and revolutionaries, out to smash the capitalist system after getting the beers in, dropping acid, speed and skinning up. Philosophers and revolutionaries one and all who made me feel like spewing. As the song says "Keep It - Que Sera Sera".

love part one

"They all dedicate lines to you. Thin lines easy seen through". Aided and abetted by Geoff Blythe's moody haunting saxophone, so begins Love Part One, Rowland's dark, cynical excursion into the complex world of love and relationships but at what cost? Reflecting on the lyrics, perhaps they are clear cut evidence of the shape of things to come, created in the mind of a twisted, tortured genius on the ascendancy.

Who knows but one thing is abundantly clear when you listen to this track. For better or for worse, to some degree or another, for the sake of love and happiness, found and lost. We've all been there, in the lyrics contained in the monologue at some point in our lives. Rowland describes a bleak landscape when it comes down to love and romance, as if he wants absolutely no part of it whatsoever or, if he does, then he appears to be emotionally ill equipped and unable to indulge in the many and varied emotions that come to the surface when love suddenly appears and knocks us for six when we're least expecting it.

And yet on the same hand, Rowland manages to hit the nail on the head when he speaks of relationships, the lies told, the price paid. How many of us have been there, caught up in the throes of a new romance and blinded by what we assume will be everlasting passion? All the lies told and promises made in earnest, expressed in the heat of the moment to impress our new love to get our own way, tricking and deceiving each other for our own ego and gratification, emotionally and financially.

How many of us have played these emotional games to the point where we dig ourselves in so deep, tied down with the trappings that come with responsibility? Desperately keeping up public appearances to family and friends, acting out our roles as a loving, caring, happy couple while deep down inside, behind closed doors, we exist in a house where love and passion no longer live. Deceiving and cheating each other in a bid to search out new love and passion with strangers. Maybe Rowland is spot on. Maybe the price many of us pay for love far outweighs the need.

there there my dear

And so we regrettably and all too quickly, arrive at the final track of the album, one of the best on offer. It begins at a blistering pace thanks, once again, to the trademark Dexys horn section blowing as one, sounding like they've been playing together for years as the soul train gathers up momentum and pulls out of the station. This time the inspiration behind the song goes back to the time in the early 80's when Dexys were touring extensively up and down the country, from theatres to clubs and student auditoriums, establishing themselves as one of the countries busiest, talented, exciting bunch of live performers and were second to none. The more times Rowland and Dexys found themselves having to deal with various student bodies, the more they started to despise their ethics. At the time many students hailed from comfortable, cosy, wealthy, middle class backgrounds and, as a result of this, they shared little or nothing in common with the working class students they came into contact with. Nevertheless, these privileged kids loved playing the working class game, fooling everybody other than themselves that they had their baby smooth, young fingers firmly on the pulse of anti-government establishment values. A transparent, fake, cop out mentality far removed from the experiences and lyrics echoed in bands like The Clash, Specials, Selector and the ever defiant socialist baird himself, Mister Billy Bragg.

And of course Kevin Rowland, who came from a poor, hardworking, Irish family himself so the lyrics contained in the song became a letter personally written by Rowland to Robin, a fictional middle class student whose false ideas, ethics and inspirations were completely destroyed by Rowland's in a broadside of cutting criticism.

The first and only time Rowland's hints to us all at his idea of a New Soul Vision but what exactly is it and when is it going to happen? The final horn section chorus builds in volume and intensity from a mere whisper to almost drowning us all in a Tsunami of loud, perfectly executed brass riffs as the train hurtles off into the distance, bidding us all a soulful farewell until the next time.

conclusions

Seconds after the album ends we sit there reflecting on the intensity and the emotions the music leaves us with, as well as a moment to catch a well-earned breath. Rowland's leaves us with a final message that gives us hope that more of the same is to come via a little sentence, telling us that everything he does is going to be funky from now on. That the 'New Soul Vision' has started in earnest, leaving us all waiting with baited breath for the next sermon in the new gospel according to preacher Rowland's, unaware that he was hatching a new plan to head off in a brand new direction with the release of the second Dexys album, Too-Rye-Ay. An album that is far removed from the music and style of Searching For The Young Soul Rebels.

Rowland's new influence, both musically and visually, was steeped in Irish folk music, adding the unthinkable idea of fiddles and violins to the horn section, mixed in with rousing, chanting lyrics and choruses. He also changed the bands totally unique, street tough, no nonsense uniform of jeans, donkey jackets, boots and skull caps for a scruffy, shoeless, rough and ready 'Raggle Taggle Gypsy Oh' image complete with long hair and bandanas, leaving us all wondering what the fuck was he thinking about by changing a nigh on perfect, original style and music on the first album, watching them perform their monster hit Come On Eileen on Top Of The Pops looking like a bunch of unemployed potato pickers.

Arguably the problem for Dexys Midnight Runners and Searching For The Young Soul Rebels and a subject raised by so many Dexys fans over the years, is that they produced a debut album that was perhaps just too good to follow up. They peaked too early with an album that should have been their third or fourth offering but that's that. There's no going back and no looking forward. It was a magical, one off moment in musical history, frozen in time. We still retain the memories and nobody or nothing can take that away from us each time we kick back and listen to Searching For The Young Soul Rebels. An album that will continue to be played by future soul music generations long after we're dead and gone, who will be moved by the same emotions contained in the music and lyrics that moved us because that is what quality soul music does. Proof enough that, despite everything else in the colourful, emotional, roller coaster career of one of the countries much loved performers, when Kevin Rowland and Dexys Midnight Runners got it right for those precious indelible forty one minutes and thirty seven seconds of musical bliss they made our world a far better place for a brief moment.

Man, did they get it spot on. End of.

mike laye

I originally got the job of photographing Dexys because I'd done some work with Bernie Rhodes for Subway Sect and The Clash. I'd sort of ended up co-managing Subway Sect with Bernie at one point, although I was really trying to build a career as a photographer.

Anyway, one day Bernie called me up and said he'd got this new band he was managing and they needed some press shots. "I want you to go down to Euston Station and photograph them, they're a right lot, they come from Birmingham and they bunk the trains all the time. And I want a picture of them jumping over the barriers".

At the time they were just about to release Dance Stance on Oddball records and the photo shoot was meant to be part of the promotional campaign.

I agreed and went down to meet this band, which I'd never heard and knew nothing else about, at Euston Station. When I arrived they were waiting for me on the other side of the barrier. There was a West Indian guy who worked for British Rail there too (you can just see his foot in the bottom of one of the shots). I went over to him and explained that I was a photographer and wanted a shot of the band jumping over the barrier. He was a bit reluctant at first but eventually gave in.

I had the band jump over the barrier several times because I could really only get one shot each time. It took too long for the flash-gun to recharge. In fact, I only managed to take four shots in all. Luckily, one of them was pretty near perfect, with Kevin Rowland leaping in the air and looking straight to camera. The guy in the middle is Bobby Ward, who was then the drummer from Subway Sect.

Once I felt I had an OK shot, I went back over to the watchful West Indian guy, thanked him profusely and shook his hand - by which point the band had exited the station. They had actually bunked the train, with my help, in the end after all!

We went outside and did some more pictures, with me still trying to work out what they were all about. What I noticed immediately was that they seemed to know each other really well and came across as a very tight unit.

There were a lot of them too, which wasn't so new to me because I'd photographed UB40 previously, but that had been like herding cats! This lot were much easier to manage. If they agreed with an idea for a shot, they would give it 100%. If they didn't, forget it. That never changed!

I took several pictures around and about Euston Station, including the one of them standing outside the Classic Hotel kebab shop. They must have decided previously that they wanted to be photographed carrying bags, one of them even has what looks like his Granddad's suitcase! But that picture is really the first, the proto-look, where they have the bags and the holdalls, even a woolly hat or two. And you can see that Kevin Archer was the one who had that look, right from the beginning. In most of the shots, Kevin Rowland is wearing a scarf, a leather hat and, I think, Geoff's long leather coat. They are pretty much all wearing DM shoes or brogues and there's a real sense of Mod style going on too. Look at Steve Spooner's suit and roll-neck and how Ivy League Bobby Ward is. Although Jimmy looks like he's been told to dress as a coalman!

Throughout this first session, all they wanted to do was be photographed looking like a gang. No, not 'a gang', that sounds scary, more like 'a team', as Geoff says. It was the band that suggested I shoot them running down the road together. Their energy, their discipline and their sense of being a team, being a group, were all very strong, right from the start. I also took that shot of them on the steps, with the band standing around and looking at Kevin Rowland, which I think is a bit of a prophetic one.

So, that Euston Station shoot was my first meeting with Pete Saunders, Pete Williams, Kevin ('Al') Archer, Big Jimmy, Steve Spooner, Kevin Rowland and Geoff Blythe, who were Dexys at that time.

My second session with the band was around the time they signed to EMI. This session was done all around Birmingham - this was The Team That Meets In Caffs session. This was how they wanted to be portrayed, because it was in a café that a lot of their planning was done and it underlined that sense of 'the team'. The photos show the pinball machines, some extreme decor and even an original Space Invaders machine in the café too.

By this point Stoker had arrived but Bernie wasn't involved any more. Dave Corke was now the band's manager. He'd called me up, told me how much he loved the pictures from the Euston Station shoot and he wanted me to do another session with them for press. So I got on the train from London and went up to Birmingham for the day.

The band took me to some boxing club in Birmingham and I got some pictures of them by the ring. They still had the bags but much smaller now (no more suitcases!), like the Adidas bags, which had that nod to the Northern Soul thing. During this shoot, I also photographed them in shops and on the top deck of a bus. On the bus with them, on the right, is Phil Sutcliffe, long-time journalist from Sounds, so some of these pictures appeared with his article. On another later session, we got some great shots on the hills overlooking the lights of the Black Country. We found a spot under a street lamp and Corky's (Dave) car had its headlights directed onto the band, too. It was dusk, almost dark, and I had the camera on a tripod. The band had to stand really still for the long exposure we needed for the shot, maybe about half a second, which is really difficult to hold. In this respect they were just great to work with. The discipline again.

I think the band really liked this shot. They liked that Birmingham was in the background and that they look like a bunch of soldiers getting ready to go or something. Their stances are so heroic.

When Geno was about to come out I got a call from Corky telling me that EMI were going to do a video for it and he wanted me to go and help out with the visuals. He was talking about the sessions on the hill and in the café and thought it would be good to represent all that in the video.

So I went to Birmingham again and took a cab to a club that Corky had organised for the video shoot. When I got there I was met by a woman from EMI International and a video guy who was going to direct the filming. It was all very low budget. It turned out that, actually, the only purpose for the video was so that the

Geno single could be promoted on European TV shows, which showed bands playing 'live'. When I introduced myself and explained why I was there, the woman from EMI said she didn't want any of this hills or caff stuff, they just wanted footage of the band playing the song live.

This hadn't been communicated to the band at all and they thought that they were doing a 'proper' pop video and had their own, very clear, ideas of what they wanted the video to be about. They told the EMI woman and the director what they wanted and, again, talked about the caff and the hill and so on, but the woman just repeated that she didn't want any of that, she just wanted the band to play live on the stage.

Well, the band didn't like this idea at all and said no, they wanted to include shots that linked them to their 'natural' environment; jumping trains, sitting in caffs and what have you. EMI woman shook her head saying no, no I don't want any of that. The argument went back and forth, back and forth, getting more and more heated, with me in the middle trying to mediate between them.

I should explain that, of course, Corky hadn't turned up. He was 'delayed on business', meaning he knew what was going to go off and wasn't taking any responsibility for it. Knowing Corky, he would have been telling both sides just what they wanted to hear and then, conveniently, been elsewhere when the shit hit the fan.

I was really getting hacked off. I'd been dumped in the middle of this stuff and it was absolutely nothing to do with me. I wasn't even getting paid to be there.

Eventually the director steps in and says OK, OK, let's stop arguing and go and get some footage of the band outside, just around the corner from the club, walking the streets, maybe in a café and so on. This cheers the band up and we get ready to go outside. But the band start muttering among themselves and on the way out of the club one of them tells me that they think the EMI woman and the director are only pretending to do this to keep them quiet and that they probably don't even have any film in the camera.

I am deputed by the band to go and demand of the director if he really does have any film in the camera. He assures me that he does and that he wouldn't pretend if he didn't. I suggest to him that he shouldn't mess the band about because they are pretty strong-willed and if they think they are being messed about it could all go horribly wrong, very quickly.

Anyway, we go outside and get some footage and the director now becomes very animated, constantly saying things like 'Great, great. We've got some great footage there, let's do this now'. Which only convinced the band even more that he really didn't have any film in the camera.

About an hour later we return to the club to continue filming the band on stage, just as the EMI woman wanted. The band take up their positions on stage and someone presses the button on a tape recorder so that they can mime along to Geno.

Now, I said that this was a 'low budget' shoot and it was, because the director only had one camera with him and he was the cameraman too! He explains to the band that, because of this, they will have to go through the song several times and each time he will be shooting it from a different position, with different lenses, to give the appearance of a multi-camera set-up.

The band nod, get ready, the playback begins and the band throw themselves into it. That was one of the strongest things about Dexys, they were always very enthusiastic and if they were into something they gave it a hundred percent. It didn't matter for them whether they played to ten people or ten thousand.

Anyway, they're miming away to the intro and it's just about to go into the first verse, and they all stop dead. They all stand there, absolutely still, just like statues. Me, the woman and the director are all looking at each, wondering what on earth is going on. But the song keeps on playing on the tape recorder and it gets to the end of the first verse and suddenly, bang, the band come to life again and carry on where they had left off, as if they hadn't even stopped.

They play as enthusiastically as normal, through until the song finishes. The EMI woman marches over to me and asks what the hell is going on. I say I have absolutely no idea. I go over to the band and ask them what's happening. They tell me that they have decided not to move during the first verse, because then EMI will be forced to use the footage they did outside.

I take this information back to the EMI woman and the director. She, of course, is furious and starts shouting that there's no way she intends for any of the outside footage to end up on the video. The director says "Well, we could mix in some of it" but the woman is adamantly refusing. The director loses his rag now, throws an artistic fit and starts yelling that he cannot work like this. I'm having to take all the flack. Where's Corky?

The woman then orders me to order them to do it again and just play the whole damn song through, properly. Again the band take their positions, someone presses play, Geno begins, the band play the introduction and again, as the verse starts, freeze absolutely still, statues again. Kevin is in some posture with his hands around the mike, Geoff, Steve and Jimmy have their instruments raised in the air and Stoker's arms are hovering over the cymbals. All frozen to the spot.

By the end of the song the woman is going absolutely ape-shit and the director is punching the air and screaming "I can't be controlled like this, I can't be dictated to like this". I'm on the phone to Bernie Rhodes, asking him for advice and if he knows where Corky is. Some chance!

In the end there were seven takes and each time the band stopped after the first verse. They point-blank refused to do anything different. The thing I totally admired was how all the band members stuck together, they were totally united in their decision. The team had agreed, nobody broke ranks and that was that. It was very impressive, and that's just what they were like on stage, too. So if you watch the video that did finally come out, you'll see that the band are playing in sync with the music for the first bit of the song, then there is all the outside stuff, with cut-aways to them on stage playing but out of sync with the music, and then the rest is them playing in sync again. The director did the best he could with what he was allowed to have!

Eventually, at about 5.30pm, Corky did show up. We all yelled at him; me, the EMI woman, the director and the band but he simply explained that he had been caught up attending to other business. Typical Corky.

I suspect that in the end EMI were pleased with the Geno video because they didn't just use it in Europe, they used it everywhere and it's still a good video.

I did another session with the band just after Geno had been released; it was commissioned by EMI to get more photos to go to the press. I think it may have been in Glasgow. They were on tour and we took some pictures on a bridge over the river. There are only seven members here (keyboard players kept coming and going) and everyone is in their woolly hats with their bags. There were pictures from this session that were featured in The Face.

By this time Dexys had their look. The Geno period was when the definition of their look came together; the woolly hats, the brogues, the leather coats and the bags. There are some nice portrait photographs of most of the band members from this period.

In the time between the first Euston Station session and the post-Geno session, the band had really evolved. They had become a lot cooler. They had time to evolve, albeit, really quickly. Kevin Rowland was wearing a red leather jacket for this session. There's a really nice picture of them down by the dockside. This was a location I took them to, mainly because I thought their look had this sort of merchant seaman element to it. To me, it was a look that signified the working man, maybe a seafaring man, definitely someone that travels. Plus, it was masculine and manly but not at all macho or threatening. They may have looked like a gang but it was not one that was going to cut your throat.

We did another big session around the time that Searching For the Young Soul Rebels was being recorded. It was in a wasteland area by the canal in Birmingham. I took loads of photographs of them there, sitting around by the canal, relaxing and posing. They wanted to be photographed like that, just hanging around. I did some other pictures of them there with an old rail tunnel as a black background. It was whilst doing this that I switched around to looking out at them from inside the tunnel and caught sight of them as silhouettes. I managed to capture some classic pictures, until they started playing 'stone the photographer'.

Later, we went up into Birmingham city centre, again just hanging around. I took one of Kevin kissing a girl but I don't know who she was. She may have been Kevin's girlfriend?

Some of the live shots are from Glasgow Barrowlands on the Intense Emotion tour. I didn't normally do a lot of live stuff. They were fantastic live, great musicians and Kevin Rowland was a very good front man. He had a way of interacting with an audience - he could be very daring and he could make people feel uncomfortable. He had a unique approach that people were not used to. He would fall to his knees, talk about emotions, stun an audience into silence and then he would build it back up into some climax. He was really an old-fashioned showman, he could be like one of those American preachers and he would work an audience in a similar way. And then to have all this backed up by the power of the brass, it was full on - it was incredible. The band could be intense and they would lift you off your feet.

This band was perfect and that's what made it all the more depressing in the end. The end was like a car crash. None of the band members have done anything as good. What Dexys had at that time was done in the right context, it just shouldn't have ended the way it did. OK, there is that James Dean element to it, but there's also that thinking, that it would have been nice to see what James Dean did next.

What was so special about the band during this period was that each person made a contribution to the band's sound – there were no side-men. Each one of them was absolutely there and each one of them added to the music. After Dexys they went on to do other good things, such as The Bureau. They wrote great songs, some of Pete Williams songs, for example, are outstanding. Kevin Archer had a lovely voice, which is much in evidence in the early demos, but he was gradually pushed out of the limelight, and what he went on to do with the Blue Ox Babes very much, shall we say, 'inspired' Kevin Rowland's song writing in the Too-Rye-Ay thing.

During my time as a photographer I went on the road with a lot of great live bands, such as The Jam and Siouxsie and the Banshees, but Dexys just swept me away. I stopped being 'professional' and became a fan. I would be down at the front with the other fans, with my donkey jacket and woolly hat, cheering the band on. I loved it because it was so powerful.

That final image is of Stoker walking away. Stoker was the most complete incarnation of the Dexys image. It's a picture that captures the lonely man. This is the image of the young soul rebel. Actually, this is the image of the end of the band. This is the image where the film freezes and the credits roll.

geoff blythe

THE NAME

When I first joined up with a bunch of guys that would eventually be known as Dexys Midnight Runners, we had no name as of yet.

I remember many days of writing and rehearsing in a garage somewhere in the suburbs of Birmingham, and talking about coming up with a name. The first version that we came up with was 'The Midnight Runners'.

Various band members have been known to give different accounts as to the derivation of that name including saying that we were poor, had to steal and then run away. Dope if you believe that one. I think, in reality, we just really liked it but we also thought that it referenced the Northern Soul scene that was powered by the music that was such an influence to us. The primary venue for this was the famed Wigan Casino, which would host all night dance parties. Bus trips had gone there from Brum and Kevin Archer (who was reputed to be adept at the gymnastic dance moves involved), was one who had availed himself of that facility. We felt, however, that we could do much better than the 'The' part of the name, thinking it should be someone's midnight runners. Various names were bandied about. Marvos was one, but eventually the brilliant idea of Dexys was hit upon. Dexys was the street term for the speed pills, Dexedrine, which was the other fuel of the (alcohol free to get round licencing laws) northern soul marathons.

And there you had it. Dexys Midnight Runners.

RECORDING THE ALBUM

The choice of Chipping Norton studios proved to be an excellent one.

A residential studio, each had his own bedroom, in the heart of the Oxfordshire countryside. We were fed two really good catered meals each day and there was an unending supply of McVitie's chocolate digestive biscuits and Hook Norton ale, both of which I, for one, availed myself of generously.

The best thing was that it was residential, so for about two weeks we had nothing to think about except for making a record. No distractions so we all became totally immersed in the project.

Also, there was plenty of space, so that sections of us that were not actually recording at any given time could work on our own parts elsewhere.

We recorded in the traditional way, bass/drums first, then at various times brass and keyboards, with vocals being done last.

Different studios have different natural sound qualities to them and Chipping Norton again proved ideal for us, with a large wooden floored, live room that naturally complemented our sound.

Of course, all of this would have been a moot point had it not been for the even more excellent decision to have Pete Wingfield produce the album. Pete, most noted for his hit Eighteen With A Bullet, was a real soul music icon in the UK, and a far sighted musician to boot. It was a perfect meeting of the minds (so much so that we also had him produce the 'Bureau' album later). He had worked with us before Chipping Norton, producing our second single (destined to be the number one hit) Geno at Tapestry Studio in London. A killer player himself, Pete also added so much to the tracks by doing a lot of the keyboard work himself, especially the slamming piano parts, as exemplified by his playing on Seven Days Too Long. It was also working on that tune in the studio that he came up with the chant/brass breakdown part in the middle of the song, helping make it so much more than just a cover song.

We had recorded the song that was to become Keep It (my best brass arrangement on the album, I think), all but the vocal, but when it came time to do that, Wingfield refused to allow Rowland's original lyric to be used. It has been said (wrongly) that it was the word fuck in the lyric that was the reason. In fact the reason was that it just sounded phonetically and rhythmically a total mess when put to Kev Archers tune. The order was then given "Someone come up with an alternative lyric". I shut myself in my room, wrote Keep It and it was recorded the next morning. Rowland, however, made it pretty clear that that he did not like singing a lyric (other than cover songs) that he did not write. It was also apparent to me and others that he had a problem having an original song on the album on which he did not have a writing credit. This problem would prove to rear its ugly head in the future.

And that is how Love Part One came to be. The discarded lyric for Keep It, I suggested to Pete Wingfield, we could do as a spoken word piece with me putting down an improvised sax part as the backdrop. It was agreed, partly because we were a little short on material, and so it became. A weird experiment for us, and a little bit of a misfit on the album, it nevertheless made the cut.

It makes me smile though to think that Rowland kind of got me back for Keep It by not giving me a writing credit on Love Part One. Hey, improvising is writing as you go along.

THE CEDAR CLUB

We obtained a residency for a while in a place called The Cedar Club, located just outside the city centre area on Constitution Hill.

The place was owned by the Fewtrell brothers of great local notoriety. It was said that a well-known T.V series at the time, which was filmed in Birmingham and entitled 'Gangsters' was loosely based on that family. At any rate, all we knew was that the brother, Chris, who ran the place, was always really good to us and fun to have a pint with at the bar.

That series of shows really got the band moving and it soon became the place to be and be seen in Brum. It started getting so packed that there would be no air left in the place. One Saturday night it was so hot that we came offstage drenched and so exhausted that we were literally sliding down the walls in our heavy coats, hardly able to stand, with our minder, Jimmy 'the Con' lifting us up and chucking us back onto the stage for an encore.

Those were really powerful shows; loud and bursting with passion and energy. A great time for us.

STEALING THE TAPES

We had the record deal with EMI which we subsequently felt was a bad one, in that it was paying a percentage that was below the norm.

We had asked Dave Corke, our manager, to re-negotiate this for us during his meetings with the company.

The timing of this was urgent, as we were gearing up to go into the studio to record the album on the back of our successes with Dance Stance and Geno. We realized, of course, that once the album was finished, EMI. would have absolutely no incentive to give us a better deal.

The time came and we found ourselves in Chipping Norton studios, with the album nearly complete and Corky telling us that the company just kept stonewalling him.

Rowland decided that our only recourse was to steal the master tapes and hold them ransom for a better deal, and so a plan was hatched.

The master tape machines were housed in a separate room from the control room to protect them from possible interference from the studio equipment. As things were finishing up, we sneaked into it and barred the door from the control room, where producer Pete and the engineer were finishing up.

What followed seemed totally 'Keystone Cops' like, with myself and others hastily winding the master tapes back, while the rest continued to block the now screaming duo in the control room from getting out of there.

It was then a bunch of us running off in all directions, with the two pro's in hot pursuit and the cops having been called.

With the help of pre-arranged getaway cars driven by friends the heist was, however, accomplished.

After many negotiations, and a marginally better deal, the tapes were eventually returned and Searching For The Young Soul Rebels was subsequently released by a somewhat chagrined EMI.

The kicker is though, that unbeknownst to us, manager Corky apparently never had been asking the company for more, and so the whole episode may have been unnecessary. At any rate, a good yarn though.

BUNKING TRAINS

We had achieved a certain notoriety as being a very anti-establishment group. That was not strictly true. Our approach was rather to do what needed to be done in whatever way it could be accomplished. That included using various 'squats' for rehearsal space and, most famously, 'bunking' trains, i.e. not paying the fare for the journey.

The latter came about mainly from us needing to travel frequently between Birmingham and London, and not having the money to afford it.

Various methods were tried and most failed. That would result in us getting a bill for the trip in the mail, at least when we could not get away with giving a false name and address when the ticket collector could not be bothered asking for identification.

Hiding in a bathroom usually did not work as the guards would check them or, if occupied, would ask for a ticket to be slid under the door.

So I came up with a system. Not free, but next best thing for a bunch of us. You buy one ticket and have everyone sit as close as possible to the bathroom. When the guard was seen approaching (you could see at least one extra carriage away), everyone except me (with the ticket) would cram into the bathroom. As he approached I would get up, get the ticket punched and in sight of him go into the bathroom and lock the door. It worked every time. We would then give it a minute or two and all pile out, most going to the bar car so that a pile of empty seats were not, all of a sudden, mysteriously occupied.

All that said, getting to an inter-city train without a ticket could be problematic, as could leaving the station afterwards. We made much of the leaving part, with our jumping the turnstile photos. Birmingham New Street was easy as they sold platform tickets for next to nothing for those wishing to see off their loved ones, or to make use of the pub on the other side of the barriers.

London Euston was more of a problem until Rowland discovered that underneath the entire station was a huge open works area packed with employees, fork lifts and the general mayhem of servicing the system.

The entrance was on a little used side street and if a couple of us at a time walked nonchalantly through it (we were already dressed for the part and often carrying a coffee or folded newspaper as a prop), no one ever seemed to notice us amongst the general hubbub. From there, there were ramps to all the platforms that came up beyond the ticket gates. Mission accomplished.

VAN MORRISON

All being fans of his, we had approached Van Morrison with a view to him producing our recordings.

We had arranged a daytime meeting with him at the Cedar Club in Brum, where we had a kind of residency. We thought we would really impress him, and thus seal the deal, if he walked into us staging a make-believe show.

The day started inauspiciously enough as, while staring out the window waiting to set up, I saw a shopping bag laden women drop to the floor as if she had been shot. So we called an ambulance. Epilepsy by all accounts.

The stage faced directly forwards to the entry doors. It was a bright sunny afternoon and we were blasting away, having been tipped off that he was about to arrive.

The doors swing open and all we can see, facing the street and the sun, is a silhouette of one little person flanked by two huge others, one on each shoulder.

In anticipation, one chair had been left in the middle of a big empty dance floor, upon which the little silhouette sits, for about thirty seconds. Nothing was said. We were still playing away, then the little silhouette gets up and the three silhouettes exit the building.

Oh well, the best laid plans of mice and soul bands.

THE 2 TONE TOUR

The Specials had been after us in one way or another for a while, whether it was using our brass section or having us on their 2-Tone label, both of which we naturally, politely declined.

The tour was pretty much ongoing when we were conscripted. A Ska thing, it originally consisted of The Specials, another Coventry ska band The Selector and the now having too much record success to play second fiddle, Madness. Hurriedly in need of a replacement, the latter having dropped out, not needing to share the limelight, we got the gig.

Most of us found that tour a blast and

we certainly cut our teeth as a live act during it. We were basically broke on that tour, it barely paid enough to keep us alive. We would get two hotel rooms for the eight band members. Each room would have two beds but by pulling the mattresses off the box-springs, we could sleep four to a room.

We certainly, on occasion, availed ourselves of the hospitality of others (unbeknown to them) in the hotel restaurants by signing our food bills to other rooms, sometimes to The Specials rooms but also to other random, unsuspecting guests. After all, we had no money to eat and the cardboard box full of slightly outdated fruit provided during sound-checks did not cut the mustard.

All three bands shared a communal tour bus. The first time we met up for this, we were the first to arrive and get on the bus. Steve Spooner and I walked down to the back of the bus and sat down on the last row of seats. Next thing we know is some big 'Rasta' dude is jumping up and down screaming at us. "Raas claat, them in me seats." We had unknowingly parked ourselves in the sacred spot reserved for trombonist Rico Rodriguez (one time bone player to the all influential ska original Prince Buster) and his trumpet playing sidekick, Dick. They were now The Specials brass section. After much crying and profuse apologies, Steve and I moved further forward up the bus. Inauspicious start to the proceedings, but all being well that ends well , we ended up on great terms with Rico and Dick, the former of whom would often give us a "little something for ourselves" at the end of a long day.

Yeah, we were the bottom of the barrel on that trip. The Selector people would make damn sure to hang around on the stage just long enough to make sure we didn't get a sound-check. We were, of course, the first band on, initially seeming really weird to the crowds we were playing to but as time went on and us becoming more known, we started to totally upstage our stage-hog friends.

Some in the band have been known to say that they did not think we were ready to take that on at that time. To me, that is B.S. We needed to jump in to the fray. To some extent, you are always ready or never ready and it is hypocrisy to go around, as we did, spouting that we had everything to say and then shy away from delivering the sermon.

That tour really cemented Dexys as the powerhouse, live unit that it was destined to become.

BERNIE RHODES

'Rehearsal Rehearsals' was a smelly, dusty, flea ridden dump in Camden Town that masqueraded as, yes, a rehearsal room.

It was owned by Bernie Rhodes, a balding, bespectacled, short chap with a penchant for wearing dirty old man type long coats and thick (very thick) soled 'brothel creepers'. He and his sidekick Mickey ('Smelly' as we christened him) Foote. I don't remember if Mickey really did have smelly feet but I have a feeling that the name didn't come out of nowhere.

Bernie was famous for having disputes with The Clash in their early days and, subsequently, The Specials. The latter were reputed to have written their, let's just say Prince Buster inspired, song 'Gangsters' about him. Bernie was well famous for the bands that had left him, as in fact, we were also destined to do.

We had to kip down there while rehearsing. We spent a lot of time on the song Dance Stance (later renamed Tell Me When My Light Turns Green on the album), as we knew that it was going to be our first single. The original version of the song was slightly too long for the basically three minute time limit that the BBC. imposed upon anything they would play on Radio 1, the main pop music channel back then. We tried many, unsuccessful, ways of cutting out those few seconds until I came up with an edit of the bridge section whilst sitting on the 'throne', a place I find many an inspiration.

We recorded Dance Stance at Chalk Farm Studios just down the road, were happy enough with the results and then, with great relief, buggered back off to Birmingham.

The next thing we know, we got a copy of the finished product, the final mix. None of us knew this was being done, assuming that we would be present at the time to oversee it. We listened to it round at my flat in Bearwood - all totally gobsmacked - we hated it. It sounded really tinny, over-compressed and was not at all the way we were envisioning our sound. We were really angry but, fait accompli, EMI. released it and basically hyped it into the top forty, giving us a really good kickstart.

Rowland went to London to confront the dynamic duo of messrs Rhodes and Foote over not getting our approval, apparently only to be told by Foote that they had no apologies and would do the same again. This insolence resulted, by all accounts, in a good 'chinning' of the man.

At any rate, that was the end of our relationship with the pair. Oh, and by the way, no, neither The Clash nor The Specials dropped in on us during that period, although a few other shady characters from the local scene did.

THE AUDITION

I had answered a 'musicians wanted' ad in the Birmingham Evening Mail, being intrigued by one of the influences quoted; Geno Washington. I had just got off the road playing with him and his perennial Ram Jam Band.

The auditions were being held at Kevin Rowland's house, where we had to go up to a bedroom and play with him and Kevin Archer. The two Pete's, Williams and Saunders, had already joined. We were trying out two songs, the soul classic Hold On I'm Coming and the ex-Killjoys original, Tell Me When My Light Turns Green.

So, I was later told, the folks were somewhat taken aback on seeing this skinny, somewhat long haired misfit walking into the room and pulling out a saxophone that seemed almost as big. Apparently, however, as soon as I started to blow the windows out with the tenor, and started chucking harmonies on stuff off the top of my head, they knew that was it.

There was already an alto sax player involved with the operation, a really nice guy with whom we stayed friends, by the name of Carl, but he was unfortunately not up to the job. I had to insist that my one condition for joining was that he had to go. This was complied with. On the same day, however, I met Steve Spooner, who was also auditioning, and immediately got on with him really well. The rest is history.

THE SOUND

The two Kev's knew that they wanted a soul style band fronted by a brass section, but neither

really had any idea of what most effectively constituted the latter and certainly not a clue as to how to arrange one musically, so that fell to me. They decided on a trumpet led section because, I suppose, that is what was most commonly seen. We had one for a while (as can be heard on the first demo's) by the name of Geoff Kent. Although I was arranging accordingly, I was really not happy with the sound. Trumpet led sections always sound like trumpet with thickening.
For reasons of which I'm unsure, Kent left and I enlisted Steve Spooner's support in insisting on keeping it as the three piece section that it had, by default, become.

The two hard blown saxes, along with Big Jim Paterson's powerful trombone playing, produced a really thick, gritty, earthy sound that freed me up to arrange the horns in the way that I had personally always heard them.
I had a unique system for arranging the brass harmonies, an approach I have not heard used by anyone else before or since, and that includes later incarnations of Dexys.

A strong part of my musical background was classical, from which I took a pretty much orchestral approach to the harmonic approach. I would work out the harmonies on paper. The trombone would hold down the bottom line but would have an aesthetically good line, not just a series of harmony notes. Steve's alto, although higher pitched than the tenor, would hold down a strong middle line, whilst I would play the lead over the top. This approach also gave me the space to improvise over the lines, if desired. Steve was a strong player but did not improvise.

I am very proud of this sound and, to this day, consider it some of my finest work.

THE TEAM THAT DREAMS IN CAFFS

The Appolonia, the goddess of greasy spoons, was down the lower end of Broad Street, pretty much opposite where Symphony Hall is now. That whole area has been long since torn down, and is now home to various eateries and naff corporate owned pubs with bad food and worse beer.

There, if not rehearsing, we would meet almost every day. Attendance was mandatory, like school, you had to be there from start time 'till dismissal.

It was a large square place with lots of tables. We always sat at the same long one by the window. We never saw many others in there, maybe a few British Rail types or construction workers on a break. Probably too late for the breakfast rush.

We must have gone through many gallons of tea there, P G Tips shares went up during that period. Occasionally a bacon sarnie when I could afford it, which I usually couldn't. Kevin Rowland usually could and, well, you would just have to drool. The owner was accepting of us, bemused I'm sure, but never gave us a hard time for the hours we spent in there.

It was HQ, the office, home away from home, where we planned, schemed or just hung out and read the paper. Our manifesto was developed there.

It is also where the two Kev's and I filmed the notorious interview for Granada TV with Tony Wilson, maven of the Manchester scene; Factory Records, etc. At that time Manchester was considered ahead of Birmingham in the dole funded band wars. This interview can still be seen on YouTube.

So the smell of that caff will always stay with me. And a bacon sandwich my greatest comfort.

RADIO

The radio bit at the start of Burn It Down was faked. Various records were used, including the German Oompah band. The choice of Specials, Pistols and Deep Purple was no accident but a snub to everything else out there. And the studio guys worked their magic to replicate the tuning in and out thing.

THE TEAM

We had described ourselves variously as a "team" a "crew" and my thing, a "tribe". We never referred to ourselves as a gang. Why? Not even that sure of that myself. I think 'gang' had too many negative connotations. We were a tribe to me because we were unique in a kind of familial sense. No one else was us, but that did not mean we thought we were not still an integral part of the outside world. As for crew and team, both are a group of people that are tied together for the purpose of achieving a specific goal. Gang does not invoke the creative and focused attitude that we had

THE LOOK

I wish I had pics of the get-ups we wore when we first hit the stage. Any Soul Rebel aficionado seeing us in that grimy ballroom of a rundown Brum hotel would be flabbergasted.

We wore totally out there costumes designed, I think with some help, by the ever fashion forward Rowland that at best made us look like the avant garde of the New Romantic movement and at worse, a bunch of somewhat effeminate B-movie superheroes.

My own outfit I described as looking like a banana republic army general after completing a coup d'état, with jodhpurs, starched white shirt with epaulets and a diagonal yellow sash, oh and of course, the sunglasses. Rowland's wore a long flowing pink creation covered by netting.

We had invited Dave Corke down to check us out with a view to representing us. He was totally impressed with the music but told us that there was no way he could not do that with us looking as we did. After all, it hardly gelled with the street soul image we espoused.

Subsequently, in a meeting to discuss the issue (we were actually at a bit of a loss as to know where to go with this) Rowland's told us that he had one more idea, and that was the New York docker look inspired by the film "On The Waterfront". This worked well for our purposes; working class tough with the right mix of romanticism and a communal identity. The hold-all type bags were part of that same style (after all, we would have looked a little off dragging multi-coloured wheely suitcases behind us).

This look suited most of us well, me personally not so much. I do not look good in a woolly hat. Initially I would wear it on the back of my head, yarmulke style, and at shows when I was doing my bending back, sax in the air thing, I found a few good shakes would make it fall to the floor where it would stay.

I then started to take a different tack, losing the hat altogether and wearing a slightly beat up, long leather coat. This became my trademark. The inspiration for this came from another film, the one that had put both Martin Scorsese and Robert De Niro on the map," Mean Streets" a 1973 film about low level New York wise-guys.

Shoes! Don't forget the shoes. It is said shoes an outfit makes and we certainly embraced that axiom, whether it was working out that the one shoe on display out in front of a Birmingham shop would have its partner on the inside display, making lifting them easy (if you could find your size) to the great hunt for the hallowed Floresheim wingtips. We were in New York in 1979 and all of us descended, late in the evening, on the still open Floresheim store. It was staffed by a solitary elderly salesman, who, not surprisingly was very nervous when we entered. Not for long though, as we all exited with a purchase, probably a week's commission in half an hour

PAUL BURTON

After a falling out with manager Dave Corke, Rowland recruited Paul Burton to fill the job.

Burton, a good Geordie lad, owned hairdressing salons, had trained Rowland as a stylist and the two had become friends.

Although Burton had no background in the music industry, the idea was that his proven business skills would be more important.

Although a really nice chap, most of us felt, however, that he had really been inducted as a yes man to Rowland at a time when he and the rest of the band were growing increasingly apart.

anthony o'shaugnassey

I was thirteen years old when that picture was taken. It was the 9th of August 1971. It was as the height of the troubles in Belfast and we lived in what was called a tenant mixed area, which was Catholic and Protestant. There was a lot of fear on both sides and Catholics were moving out to live in Catholic areas and Protestants were moving out to go and live in Protestant areas. But we were not going to move and what had happened was that some Protestants had set fire to our houses. Unfortunately the fire brigade couldn't get up the street so we had no choice but to flee. So what you see in my arms is basically all that I could grab. In the little suitcase was a two-bar electric fire and my pride and joy, which was my Subbuteo and a couple of cars. In the other bag were my pyjamas and one set of clothes.

The area where the picture was taken was called Cranbrook Gardens in North Belfast. It was around 4 o'clock in the afternoon. There is a young boy wearing a duffle coat on the left hand side, that was my brother Kevin, and then on the right hand side there is a another boy wearing shorts, that was my brother Gerard.

At the time there was shooting going on above our heads. The Catholics were firing because they were worried about the Protestants coming further into their area, so they were firing warning shots. You can't really see in the picture but there's a coal lorry and in front of it there is (what were called) Saracens and they were returning fire. That's why the older boy (holding Gerard's arm) is kind of bowing down.

I didn't know the photograph had been taken until the next day, when we came back and our house was gone - nothing left of it at all. I had a neighbour from across the street and he told me that he had been to work in London and he had seen the picture in the London Evening Standard. I have never actually seen it.

Then in 1980 a friend of mine told me that he had seen a photograph of me on an album. I thought he was joking or that it was somebody that just looked like me, so we went to the record shop where the record was plastered all over and there was also a full-scale cut-out of the cover with me on it. I can still, more or less, feel now what I felt then - WOW! Everything was going round and round in my head. I remember pointing out the woman in the background and saying that it was my mum. I couldn't buy the album at the time because I didn't have the three bob on me but I did eventually get a copy. I also met the band too. Geno was out, had continued into the summer when the band came to Ireland and we got tickets. Whilst we queuing up outside there were a couple of security and roadies and they were wearing tee-shirts with my face on it. So I went up to one of the women and told her that it was my face on the tee-shirts. I don't think she really believed me but she told me to come back after the show and she would take me to the hotel where the band were staying. I took a copy of the cover that I had picked up and I got it signed by the band (and I've still got it). I remember talking to Kevin Rowland, Geoff and Jim Patterson.

neil sheasby

That album was like a religion for me. As was Sound Affects but that was album was totally different. I first came across them when I was only about twelve. I saw them doing Dance Stance on Top of the Pops. Like a lot of people, I think I just kinda lumped them in with the Two Tone thing and the mod revival. So at that time I didn't think any different of them as those other bands. The only thing was they looked different. They (Dexys) really intrigued me and then Geno came along. What was more they were on my doorstep; they came to play at Tiffanys in Coventry and I tried to get in. The Specials and The Selecter were also playing but I was too young to be let in.

Then when the album came along I realized that they were not like all those other bands. There was even something about the album sleeve that looked different. Even then you could tell that they stood aside and they seemed to just refuse to sit in a pigeon hole. I could see that they wanted to distance themselves from the sort of mod and ska thing - I really liked that and it was something that really drew me in.

So I played the album and it completely blew me away, and it was like nothing I had heard before. Even the sleeve notes were part of it and all that; the essays, the lyrics and the caper stuff. They presented things really well and I found them to be a more serious and considered affair. Their attention to detail was just stunning.

The Jam made me want to be in a band, play bass and get my own Rickenbacker but it was the Searching For The Young Soul Rebels that made me stop and think. I would find myself asking 'what would Kevin Rowland do?'.

It also felt like I had found something that was my own and that no one else had found. I remember seeing a few kids dressing like the band; woolly hats and leather coats but that look seemed to move on very quickly. But the Dexy thing stuck with me for a long time and I really got it intensely.

The next year (1980) I went back to Tiffanys and this time I got in. But I remember spending much of the time feeling worried that I was going to get kicked out - I was still only thirteen. The gig was intense. It was a complete blast at you. By this time I had seen both Madness and The Specials live but the Dexys gig was completely off the scale. I had seen The Jam, The Beat but Dexys were completely different. It was a small venue and I was packed in with loads of people. That gig changed everything for me.

There was also something about that gig that made it feel like a punk gig. It had that vibe to it. They (band) didn't seem to give a fuck whether the audience was there or not. They weren't there to crowd please. It was more like 'we know we're good, this is it and we don't give a fuck!' There was no showbiz, there was very little communication and I left the gig asking myself 'what the fuck was that?' It was just great. 'Searching' was the soundtrack to my life at that time and then six months later they were gone and Dexys had reinvented themselves (hooded tops and boxing boots) into something else and that was that.

Rowland singing about the searching for the soul rebels was my calling. I mean I was only young, I was just starting a band and I was thinking he (Rowland) is singing about us. It was complete inspiration. I loved Rowland's vision for the band. You had people coming to soul music through Motown and Stax records and, to a degree, northern soul and then you had this band from Birmingham doing versions of Seven Days Too Long and Breaking Down the Walls of Heartbreak and it was brilliant. It just didn't feel like it was being done in a retrospective way but it was bringing something new to it. It was like Dexys were saying 'this is what those records sound like but this is what we like sound like'.

I didn't have many friends who were into them (Dexys). Geno was popular but it was mainly me and my friend Hammy (Paul Hanlon) who got obsessed by them. I played in a band with Hammy for several years and our band was called Dance Stance. Me and Hammy knew of each other but we became proper friends after he clocked me one day holding a copy of the Rebels album. That album was the big bond between us. We were inseparable for the rest of his life. We actually met Kevin Rowland when we were still kids but we never ever had the balls to tell him we had a band called Dance Stance.

We played the 30th anniversary show in Birmingham after a conversation with Ian Jennings. At first we said no because Ian asked us to play a couple of songs from the album. We said we just couldn't do the songs justice and believed the songs were uncoverable. And we didn't want to do a version of Seven Days Too Long either. Then Ian said 'oh that's a shame because Big Jim and Geoff said they would have played with you'. At this point Big Jim hadn't played his trombone for something like sixteen years. So I said to Ian 'hold on leave it with me', I wasn't gonna let that go.

Stone Foundation got together and had a think about how we could do it. We decided we would learn Tell Me When My Light Turns Green and I Couldn't Help It If I Tried. They actually worked and we even went on to record I Couldn't Help It If I Tried with Joe Harris. We sent the demos to Geoff and Jim. They really liked them and it went from there.

We didn't actually meet until the day of the sound check (in the Flapper and Firkin) and that was something else. Sandra (Jims' wife had tears in her eyes). Before the gig he had been sending me emails telling me how nervous he was and he didn't know if he could do it, didn't know what to wear, wasn't sure how he would be. And then in the sound check it was just amazing. There's some footage on YouTube of us all playing Tell Me When My Light Turns Green. It was a special night and all the band were there apart from the two Kevin's and Stoker. And from there Big Jim has returned to playing with Kevin Rowland again on the latest album.

I consider Searching For The Young Soul Rebels album to be the greatest debut album of all time. It was totally unique. It didn't follow any rules. There were not conformist in any way and they had a great gang look. It blew me away.

drew hipson
editor

ALL MOD ICON MAGAZINE

So a second time they (the Pharisees) called the man who had been blind, and said to him, "Give glory to God we know that this man is a sinner."

He then answered, "Whether He is a sinner, I do not know: one thing I do know, that though I was blind, now I can see."

So they said to him, 'What did He do to you? How did He open your eyes?"

John IX. 24–26, The New English Bible.

Back in the eighties, Searching For The Young Soul Rebels was much more than just an album, to me it was an almost religious-like experience. It was about meeting other 'big shot boys' in caffs and plotting a 'small town' escape, cleansing your soul with late night running and searching for purity of spirit. The album sleeve - which unbeknown to me at the time, depicted an Irish family being uprooted during the 'troubles' - conveyed spiritual unrest, and the iconic shot of drummer Andy 'Stoker' Growcott - with his On The Waterfront clobber and kit-bag - had the same impact on me as the lone image of Robert De Niro in the cinema poster for Martin Scorsese's Taxi Driver. The inner sleeve notes, which told of the 'team' recruiting members, secretly listening to Stax and rehearsing for the 'big one' that was about to go 'off in the Midlands', read like a crime syndicate plot, and gave the impression that the band were a group of 'wildhearted outsiders', readying to take on the music business. It was all so intoxicatingly cinematic.

Front man Kevin Rowland would cite several movies as inspiration – John Schlesinger's Midnight Cowboy and Martin Scorsese's Mean Streets and Raging Bull. These films focused on male bonding on a spiritual level, and in the case of the latter two films, the underlying motif was the pursuit of spiritual redemption. It would come as no surprise to later learn that, like Scorsese, Rowland had considered a vocation in the priesthood.

Although guitarist Kevin 'Al' Archer was a pivotal member of the 'firm', co-writing the two singles Geno and There, There, My Dear, and composing one of the album's finest moments, The Teams That Meet In Caffs, it was the overpowering drive and contrary madness of maverick front man Kevin Rowland which lent the album much of its power. The opening statement of intent features a radio broadcast which tunes in and out of snippets of Deep Purple, the Sex Pistols and The Specials, ending with Rowland dismissing them all in favour of his 'new soul vision'. Rowland had already sneered at Sex Pistols frontman Rotten, with his own punk outfit The Killjoys, and their debut single Johnny Won't Get To Heaven, the title of which, incidentally, would hint at his new musical vision of Punk fury, mixed with spiritual Soul. Rowland's call to arms, and the band responding as if collectively psyching themselves up for the fight, summed up the team spirit and the singular mood of defiance which would permeate the album. The opening track Burn It Down set the tone, with Rowland angrily railing against those who still perpetuated anti-Irish sentiments. Aside from the power of the horns, most notable was the brilliantly fluid bass work of Pete Williams, which essentially was the backbone of the album, and Andy Growcott's sensationally precise and intelligent drumming. In fact, although contractually the band were a 'nucleus' of three, credit must be given to the astonishing musicianship of all of the members who played on the album, most notably alto sax player Steve 'Babyface' Spooner, trombonist Big Jimmy Paterson (who co-wrote the breath-taking Blues Jazz epic I Couldn't Help If I Tried) and tenor sax player Geoff 'JB' Blythe (formerly of Geno Washington's Ram Jam Band), who co-wrote I'm Just Looking and Keep It.

Although Searching For The Young Soul Rebels was not a concept album in the conventional sense, there was a definite collective vision and lyrical thrust. The band were not only taking on the existing musical order, they were also attacking left-wing trendies and the 'hippy press'; There There My Dear questioning existing notions of love, Love Part One appealing for kindred spirits to share the 'new soul vision', I'm Just Looking, I Couldn't Help If I Tried and, searching for spiritual salvation in the face of convention, Keep It, Thankfully Not Living In Yorkshire It Doesn't Apply and Tell Me When My Light Turns Green. The latter song was essentially Rowland's Pilgrims Progress and would chart the restless soul searching that would continue throughout much of his life. The concept of penance in the pursuit of spiritual redemption (which referenced the religious conflict of Harvey Keitel's character Charlie in Mean Streets) was furthered with the inclusion of a quote from the Old Testament Psalms next to the track listing.

Musically the band asserted that they had been listening to Cliff Bennett, Zoot Money, James Brown and Aretha Franklin, and had covered Sam & Dave's Hold On, I'm Comin' and Chuck Wood's Seven Days Too Long – the latter of which would end up on the album. The source of inspiration was not unique in itself, as the musical climate in the UK at the time had shifted from Punk and post-Punk to Soul and Funk, with many bands including or enlisting a brass section, which, more often than not were older session musicians. However, the difference with Dexys Midnight Runners was that they were an 'eight handed' outfit; they didn't use session musicians because the two sax players and the trombonist were actual band members. They dressed in the collective gang attire and were an integral part of the 'team', contributing to and co-writing the music. This was one of the things that set the band apart from their contemporaries and made them so unique.

One journalist, reviewing the album, criticised the fact that the brass parts were, according to him, all in the wrong places. For me though, this was one of the album's strengths; not that the brass parts were necessarily in the wrong places, but the fact that they were used in a more unorthodox manner and closer to the style and tone of a film score. A case in point is the track I'm Just Looking, which utilises stabs of brass in a manner that is similar to the melodramatic bursts of saxophone used to such great effect by film composer Bernard Herrmann in his score for Taxi Driver.

One of the most cinematic tracks on the album is the stirring four minute masterpiece The Teams That Meet In Caffs, which features Pete Williams' best bass work, shimmering organ passages by Pete Saunders and has a melody that attains the beauty and grandeur of John Barry's Midnight Cowboy theme. The piece was composed by Kevin Archer, who would later pen the equally brilliant post-Dexys instrumental The Last Detail with his band The Blue Ox Babes.

In the early eighties, inspired by Searching For The Young Soul Rebels and seventies road movie Scarecrow, myself and two other 'small town big shot boys' did escape. We packed our kit bags and boarded a bus in Glasgow, on a rainy night when the blurring lights of the bus station flashed in and out of focus Taxi Driver style. We absconded to London, then to Calais and on to Paris, where we were caught trying to bunk the train and subsequently fined. In Dijon, in a moment of Dexys inspired bravado, we jumped a freight train and ended up, hours later, several miles outside of Marseille. It was all part of the caper. As winter set in we found ourselves holed up in Annecy, South-East France, virtually penniless and sleeping in an underground car park. Most evenings were spent sitting in a local cafe playing cards and planning our next move, with vacuous french muzak playing in the background. On one particular night, we were contemplating whether to look for work in Switzerland or make our way back to London, when suddenly, and seemingly out of nowhere, The Team That Meet In Caffs came blaring out of the radio. It was a sign, we knew it. The first part of the caper was over. We packed our bags and began the journey back to London.

Since its release, Searching For The Young Soul Rebels has lost none of its power and still has the ability to inspire. Back then it was our 'bombers', our 'Dexys', our 'high'. It instilled in us a sense of self-discipline, gave us spiritual strength and urged us to keep 'searching'. In over thirty years, little has come close to the incendiary power and spiritual impact of this incredible album, and for that I am eternally thankful to Kevin and 'The Team'.

peter jachimiak

Dexys Midnight Runners' Searching For The Young Soul Rebels – Speed, Stevedores and Spirituality.

Like a parliament of night owls, they seemed to be on permanent, conspiratorial night shift. Their name reflected this. Dexys Midnight Runners; Amphetamine-fuelled, nocturnal, fast-paced, forward movement. Thus, they demanded, 'Tell me when my light turns green'. Rolling with Kevin Rowland and his '79 crew, with holdalls in hand or slung over shoulders, they prowled alleys and backstreets, seemingly always on the paranoiac edge. When they did sit still, they sat upon the tops of formica tables, just like 'The team that meet in caffs'. Possessed by the troubles in Northern Ireland and infuriated by the Irish being the butt of all jokes, there, amid the dripping HP Sauce bottles and overflowing metal ashtrays, they entered into an intense, emotional form of Soul exorcism. Heads bowed, hands clapping and fingers snapping, theirs was a nigh-on spiritual quest. They were, after all, collectively Searching For The Young Soul Rebels. As Kevin Pearce, in Something Beginning with O insisted, Dexys' "quasi-religious, cathartic, cleansing aspect", whereby Rowland was "purging himself so in song, allows the listener to be emotionally involved and spiritually renewed". Thus, in 1980, they energetically embarked on their 38-date 'Straight To The Heart' tour, emotionally involving and spiritually renewing all as they went their way.

Dodging fares by leaping over turnstiles, Dexys – who were always glancing nervously over their clutch of broad shoulders – came across like petty hoodlums who had just raided the local drugstore. They did their time by endlessly listening to music, selecting the right tunes, 'Breaking Down The Walls Of Heartache', 'Hold On! I'm Comin'', 'Respect', 'Seven Days Too Long', 'Soul Finger', and, proudly displaying a veneer of criminal glamour, they were, at the very least, guilty of stealing the master tapes of their own debut LP from EMI.

But, first, there was 'the look'; as a teenager who had grown up in northwest London during the late 1960s, Kevin Rowland aspired to be a 'Top Mod' amid a swelling sea of 'Peanuts' to be found in and around Harrow, Wembley and Willesden. So, pre-caricature Skinhead, he embraced this all-American look of single-breasted, fly-fronted raincoats, V-neck sleeveless sweaters, Sta-Prest and wing-tip Royals. With the militaristic style of both astronauts and GIs in the mix, and with a sophisticated sprinkling of Ivy League on Madison Avenue, to Rowland "this was the great lost look". As, indeed, Rowland later prophesised that "before long, a new kind of short hair would be back". Thus, it was 'the look' that gave the first incarnation of Dexys, albeit in a post-Punk bastardised manner, their image not quite Mod, nor Two Tone, they were, instead, grown-up 'Peanuts' with grown-out crops. No wonder that Dexys' tenor saxophonist Geoff 'JB' Blythe, dismissing the notion that they were just 'a band', later asserted, "A tribe would be a better word, a small tribe".

There was 'the look'; black, three-buttoned suit jackets with slim lapels, (sometimes in leather), donkey jackets, roll-necks, pencil moustaches, wrap-around shades and woollen skull caps. With their front-man known by the Romany-esque nom de plume Carlo Rolan around this time, these were working-class gigolos who looked as though they had been out of town for a year or two due to a forced vacation at Her Majesty's pleasure and were now scraping by, working as stevedores down the docks of New Jersey.

Finally, there was 'the look'; backs up against metal shutters or bare brickwork and Woodbines perched on lips, this dour-faced firm stared out at us intently with piercing eyes. A muscular, physical brass section at their heart, they'd offer us out if they only thought we were hard enough to take them on. No, instead, 'I'm just looking'. For, countering their hard image, Rowland, in an interview with Record Mirror's Colin Irvin, asked "Did we have an image of a lean mean fighting machine?" Rowland went on to answer his own question with typical philosophical honesty, "I thought we looked more romantic or spiritual".

Nevertheless, coming across in their press shots like extras from a Scorsese film, the black-and-white photographs by Mike Laye, with their air of documentary realism, made Dexys Midnight Runners look as though they were conducting auditions for eventual mugshots. Thus, in a way, Laye's snapshots of maverick Rowland et al. transformed a mere New Wave pop group into eventual icons of British Streetstyle Noir.

Come 1981, and the next incarnation of Dexys was just as overtly masculine, perhaps even more ultra-physical. Wearing boxing boots and hooded tops, with their hair long in pony tails, the emphasis was now upon training, discipline, and mental purity. Singing in harmony, and jogging en masse at night under the glow of streetlights, this was their new 'Dance Stance'. This, then, was to be the true loneliness of Rowland's long-distance runners…

Politicised. Passionate. Pure. With always a 'Plan B' to hand. Dexys Midnight Runners would forevermore be soulful rebels with a cause; rebels who were on a never-ending search for the near-elusive sweaty, sacred spirit of a '68 'Geno'.

Sources:
Daryl Easlea (2010) sleeve notes to the 30th anniversary special edition of Dexys Midnight Runners' Searching For The Young Soul Rebels, EMI Records.
Paul Gorman (2001) The Look – Adventures in Pop & Rock Fashion, London: Sanctuary.
Kevin Pearce (n.d.) Something Beginning with O, London: Heavenly.
Richard White (2005) Dexys Midnight Runners – Young Soul Rebels, London: Omnibus.

eddie cooney

I got into Dexys with Geno. I was really lucky in that my brother told me about this great record before it hit the charts. He was in the RAF in Shawbury, Shropshire and I went to visit him for a few days. After he'd left home I missed him. We should have been out getting pissed together, courting girls, normal growing up stuff and now he was gone. Something told me he wouldn't be back. He taught me the song, not formally, he just sang it out loud at every opportunity and eventually I joined in. Our version of Geno was sung out loud in various areas of Shrewsbury and its outskirts. By the end of my visit I knew all the words to the song and didn't even have a copy yet! Dexys and Geno became an intrinsic part of my life and some of the glue that bonded my relationship with my brother. We were able to watch Geno gradually climb the chart (it entered the British chart at number 61!) and eventually hit number one. It was a really exciting time. I still love Geno but when I heard Dexys' version of Breakin' Down The Walls Of Heartache on the b-side I just knew they were something special.

I'd always had my own personal view of what constitutes soul music and here it was, really passionate but serious and meaningful. I played both sides of that single over and over again. Then I read in a magazine that Geno was their 2nd single. I couldn't believe that I'd missed a single. I rang my brother but he didn't know anything about it. We tried for weeks and failed to get Dance Stance. It had been such a small hit that all the copies had sold out and then it was deleted so impossible to order. I went on holiday to Germany (I have family there) and in Köln (Cologne to foreigners) there is a massive railway station with a market below ground. I was lazily looking through a pile of singles and came across about 10 copies of Dance Stance. YES! I just KNOW that I was meant to find them. I wouldn't have even been looking if my train hadn't been late. Then I had to wait two whole days before I got home and was able to play it. I got a copy for my brother, of course. What a song! You had to have an IQ to understand it. Even if you did manage to work out what the song was about it probably insulted you. Everybody I'd ever met told jokes about the Irish, resorted to the weak, hostile, ultimately racist view that they were thick, stupid. I'd never thought about how humour could be hostile before this moment listening to Dance Stance, it was educating me. Wow! This definitely wasn't any ordinary group. I never told another racist joke of any kind after Dance Stance. Only personal politics maybe, but who says music can't change things? We were only two singles in. How can a band become your all-time favourite after two singles? What if they didn't mean it? This became a crucial thought. What if they didn't mean it? I had to see Dexys for myself. The music press didn't help. I'd already worked out that they were Liars A to E.

It was a cold spring night in 1980 when I went to see Dexys Midnight Runners. Our breath froze in the air. With me was a French girl, Yolande Baillon, what ever happened to her? I'd only met her for the first time the week before. Now I was meeting her off a bus in Lord Street, Liverpool and taking her to see Dexys. We walked to the club, arms around each other to keep warm. She'd never heard of them. I tried to explain. When I used the word 'soul' she went off on a tangent. 'What like… Stevie Wonder? or Diana Ross.' 'No, No, not like them,' I said. 'Like Marvin Gaye then?' 'No, no, not even like Marvin Gaye.' 'Who are they like? They must be like someone.' 'Maybe like Geno Washington. Have you heard of him?' 'No, what is he like?' 'I've no idea.' She laughed at me, 'Crazy Englishman.' 'Yeah, crazy' and I laughed too. The club was dingy. The carpets stuck to your feet. It smelt of damp, stale tobacco and spilt beer that hadn't been cleaned up. We were early, there were only about 100 people there. I never counted heads but I don't think many more people turned up. Quite soon the support group were on. The Upset featured one Archie Brown on vocals and occasional sax. He had a weird rasping voice, it squealed and strangled itself around the vocals. I liked them. They were powerful, angry and soulful. It was going to be a good night. An hour passed after the Upset had played. Where were Dexys? I had to get home on the bus. I was on the dole and didn't have enough money for a taxi. Then onto stage ambled a lone figure, it took a while to realise he was telling jokes. The audience were getting restless. A few shouts of

'Geno, Geno, Geno' started. I thought he was funny and tried to listen. The 'Geno' brigade wandered off to the bar and about 50 people were left standing in front of the stage. The comedian started telling a joke about shagging a donkey (no, really!) which got a few sniggers. He was trying to shock with obscenity but it wasn't working. He was staring into the audience, looking at each face in turn. He settled on me and we looked into each other's eyes. He stopped telling the donkey joke and shouted, 'There! There's someone who's listening!' 50 people were all looking at me now. 'What's your name?' 'Eddie.' 'Come up here Eddie.' Quick as a flash I said the only thing possible, 'No,' and the comedian just as quickly went on with the joke. I was quite impressed that he wasn't at all phased by his inability to extract a village idiot from the audience. But my 'no' had been final and he knew it. There was no way I was being made to look like a twat tonight of all nights. Of course, several things went through my mind in that split second. Including, 'I might get to meet the band.' The comedian's name? Keith Allen. We waited another hour, at least, before Dexys arrived on stage. It looked like I would be walking home. I remember thinking that they had better be worth it. They were incredible. Like nothing else. I really, really loved it. The stage entrance was so quick it took everyone by surprise. There was a blast of hot air from the brass. You could actually feel it. The 'Geno' brigade rushed back from the bar and started to shout mid-song 'Geno, Geno, Geno,' immediately there was a tension between band and audience. At first they were ignored but you could tell the band were pissed off. Then I noticed Al (Kevin) Archer pointing threateningly into the crowd. He was arguing with someone in the 'Geno' brigade. Maybe this had happened before, at other venues. The first few songs were a blur. I don't know what they opened with. It was definitely an instrumental. Maybe, The Teams That Meet in Caffs. I mostly remember smiling a lot, thinking, 'Yes! They mean it! They actually mean it!' Most memorable song was Thankfully Not Living In Yorkshire. It was a weird venue with loads of false columns all around the place. The tiny stage (too small for the band) had rows of columns on either side of the stage to the bar at the back, so whoever was on stage couldn't see left or right. This clearly pissed off Kevin and before the song he said, 'I don't know what's going on over there (pointing left) and I don't know what's going on over there (pointing right) but right here (pointing to the floor) is pure soul.' Then he started to sing the falsetto verses. The larger part of the audience started to laugh but Kevin (who had noticed) just carried on singing. His concentration was immense and his performance, well, fantastic. There are no adequate superlatives. When he got to the 'Ooh ooh a a' chorus the whole audience was hooked, including those who'd laughed. Everybody dancing and singing 'Ooh Ooh a a.' Actually, at this point it struck me as funny that 200 or so people were singing 'Ooh ooh a a' out loud. By now the 'Geno' brigade were pissing me off too. There was no let up. 'Geno, Geno, Geno' between every song. I'd only heard the 4 songs from the singles before the concert. I wanted to listen, dance and sing. Kevin had been telling them to fuck off. 'No, we're not playing it, fuck off!' 'It's boring now, fuck off.' He was really aggressive towards them and, I swear, they were scared. Eventually they gave up and stopped shouting about 10th song in, then and only then Kevin said, 'This is for those people who were here last time we played in Liverpool. Only 10 people came to see us.' The band started shouting, 'Geno, Geno, Geno' and all of those who had waited for it were suddenly delirious. The whole performance had been really tense, you felt that violence could spark at any moment. The tension was turned into sheer adoration. Kevin was so focussed he verged on possessed. During Geno he played a guitar and at one point hit Pete Williams, who was standing next to him, on the head with the guitar neck. There was blood, I think, but Kevin didn't notice and kept playing. Pete had doubled over in pain but got up again and carried on. At the end of the song someone (JB, I think) pointed out what had happened and Kevin went to see if Pete was OK. Kevin was really concerned, talking to Pete and the gig stopped for a few minutes. I didn't think Pete was OK but they carried on anyway. Kevin went to the mike and waited. 'Geno, Geno, Geno.' 'Oh no,' I thought. We'd had Geno, it was enough. But this time Kevin just said, 'Ssshhh' and waited. He put his hands up to the mike. His hands were open but the fingers closed tightly together, pointing upwards, shielding the microphone. 'Ssshhh,' 'Ssshhh.' Eventually, silence… and the brass started, low, mournful but again powerful, 'You gave me your ace card, I gave you my time…' It was sheer, fucking brilliance. When he got to the chorus, 'If there is someone, point out that someone, who thinks like I see, who thinks just like me.' I was thinking, maybe shouting out loud, of course there was someone, it was me! Me! I'm here! My eyes welled up with tears. Then they were gone. People were calling out for an encore. 'Geno, Geno, Geno.' 'Oh for fuck sake! That's not going to get them back on stage.' They had to come back on. It couldn't be all over. Then the French girl said that she had to go home. Oh no, I'd forgotten all about her. She had to get up early the next day. I had to go with her. The band might come back on. I couldn't say no. This was Liverpool. At night. It took a few minutes to find a taxi for her. Yes, it was OK I had enough money for a taxi home. Liar. I rushed back to the club but people were coming out. They'd played an encore, 2 songs and I'd missed it. I didn't want to know the details.

I suddenly realised that I was freezing cold, soaked with sweat and had a 10 mile walk ahead of me. As I was walking home I couldn't work out what I'd seen. I hardly noticed the walk. Haven't got a clue what time I got home. I thought about the concert all the way. For days after I kept remembering bits, flashes of images like photographs. It sounds stupid, doesn't it? But it's true. Some of those images I still remember today. That night is still imprinted on my brain. I was hooked. I'm still hooked but the quality of everything that has come from the Dexys' stable is enormous. So far so good, eh? Love to all who feel just like me.

gerrard saint

'As an art director my job is to organise that sort of visual world in the sense that you feel that you are stepping into the world of the band. I mean you could sort of show anything so it's about the choices about how you do it. And that first Dexys album just felt like the bands world. It captured that whole gang thing.'

paolo hewitt

I was working for Melody Maker and went to interview the Nips. They were playing at the Music Machine and the other band on was a band that I hadn't heard of called Dexys Midnight Runners. So I went down to the Music Machine and saw the Nips and then Dexys Midnight Runners came on and they 'fuckin' blew me away'. I know it's an old cliché but they were just so powerful. The horns were just like phoar - incredible. And Kevin was doing his various moves. After that I went to see them loads and I remember Kevin would do this part where he would go 'Big Jimmy, Big Jimmy drinks half a bottle of scotch a day, play something Big Jimmy, play something for me'. Kevin and the band were drama on stage.

I went to interview them up in Wales. They were on tour. And I'm with them on the train and they wouldn't talk to me. Instead I read a book. That's what they were like. Dexys were saying that soul music is about an expression of feelings. They were telling people that they were playing soul but they weren't trying to be Otis Redding. They were trying to do something that would reach people in its own soulful way. Which they did! The songs from that album (Soul Rebels) still stand up today.

simon franklin

That album was a kinda of a mould breaker in every sense. I mean the band took its name from one of the 60's mod drugs of choice for a starter. It had a pure modernist sound too, taking its influences from bands that mods followed like Jimmy James and Geno Washington, which amongst the mod revivalists weren't so obvious and not so accessible. The title sat nicely and was like the Impressions 'A Young Mods Forgotten Story', a statement of intent. I'm not sure too many of the revivalists at the time got it. They were certainly a band a band with their own clique or gang, especially the way they dressed like something from the Marlon Brando film 'On the Waterfront', all donkey jacket, woolly fisherman's hat and monkey boots. Personally IO loved this, it appealed to my journey for authenticity and originality. Nobody played this kind of passionate soul music, at least no one who came from Birmingham. I'm not sure even The Jam were as passionate about following their art form to the extremes that Dexys did or did anybody wear their heart on their sleeves as much. As for the music it was difficult and slightly challenging, all music that preaches and has a message is, but it was also tuneful, the mark of a great song smith. I can only think of a few other artists who careers have followed similar paths to Kevin Rowland, I mean after this album, I'm not sure any of us were ready for what came next…

neil warburton

I was about nine year's old when I brought my first record in 1980, and that first record I brought was Geno by Dexys Midnight Runners. The horns just literally blew me away, and what a B-Side – a cover of Johnnny Johnson and The Bandwagon's 1968 hit 'Breaking Down The Walls Of Heartache'. Apparently EMI wanted this to be the A-Side instead of Geno, it was a guaranteed No. 1, Geno hit No.1 anyway and as they say 'the rest is history.' I loved Dexys hard-man stance with their donkey jackets and woolly hats, oh and 'Dexys Midnight Runners' – what a great name for a band (or 'group' should I say?) I thought. It was months later until I found out what it actually meant! And who was this Geno guy anyway? Years later I ended up interviewing him in his hotel room for the unofficial Dexys fanzine 'Keep On Running'!

I have never stopped playing it to this day. I remember thinking at the time how individual it seemed to sound compared with other music that was around at the time. As time went on I was also warming to the fact that nobody else I knew seemed to like them (I've always been a bit of a loner so this suited me just fine). I found this strange, especially with Rowland being a local lad, years later I began to realise that most of these people were just jealous of his success.

I'd missed Dexys debut single Dance Stance (re-titled Burn It Down on Searching) that just crept into the charts at No.40 (but still managed an appearance on Top Of The Pops though), but luckily enough I managed to pick it up in a second-hand shop just around the corner from me on Rood End Road. Carlo Rolan? Anyway, just after I had Geno in my grasp, a few days later they were on Top Of The Pops, I watched this with my parents and when Dexys came on I could not believe it when my Mum turned round to me, looking very surprised, and said something like – "He only lives up the road", 'up the road' did not mean about two miles away or something, it actually meant about ten doors away. I could not believe it, here I am, just brought my first record and I'm told that the lead singer lives up the road!

So, as you can probably guess, the next morning I'm knocking his door, holding my copy of Geno tightly to me. What I was dreading happened – no bloody answer, I walked home with my head down – there's always tomorrow I thought. When I did finally get round to seeing him they had just released There There My Dear and they were on Tiswas on the Saturday morning performing this, I went round his house that very evening and he was in. I could not believe it when he opened the door, I said something like (all of a panic) - "Can I have your autograph please, I seen you on Tiswas this morning", he seemed quite pleased that I had seen him on the TV that morning and invited me into his house. He asked me where I lived and so on, not knowing to me beforehand, I had actually seen Kevin walking down the road on numerous occasions (I can always remember him spitting a lot!). Kevin signed Geno for me and also gave me a signed photo of the band on Top Of The Pops – which is now framed and holds centre-stage in my front room.

From that day on Kevin always acknowledged me when we crossed paths walking down the street (remember the thumb routine Kev?). If it was raining Kevin would be walking down the street with a newspaper or plastic bag over his head! I suppose him walking down the street with an umbrella wouldn't have suited the Dexys hard-man image at that time!

The debut album Searching For The Young Soul Rebels arrived in July of 1980. With me still being a little innocent 9-year old school-boy I had to wait until the Saturday for my Mum to take me to Birmingham with her on the bus to pick it up. After it was in my grasp, I couldn't wait to get home to hear it, so I duly played up in Birmingham to get home as soon as possible! I studied the album during the bus journey back – Who's that on the cover? Is that a young Carlo? Years later I would discover that the picture is that of an original photo taken during the Belfast riots of 1971, with people fleeing their burning homes in Cranbrook Gardens. The guy at the centre of that photo is a young Anthony O'Shaughnessy, he was tracked down by Ian Jennings for the 30th Anniversary of Searching For The Young Soul Rebels event which was held in Birmingham in 2010. During Dexys recent tour in 2013, I had the pleasure of being in Anthony's company for a weekend in Ireland where he showed me where that now famous photo was taken.

Anyway, I continue to study the album on the bus journey home and take out the inner-sleeve notes, which are printed on a thick white card (meticulously produced as with everything that Dexys have ever produced). I began to read – 'On a hot night in July 78 two men, Kevin Rowland and Al Archer left their low-profile Birmingham hide-out to round up a firm of boys...' I was hooked and intrigued straight away and I hadn't even got home to play the record yet! Where was this 'Birmingham hide-out'? Was it the Apollonia Cafe on Broad Street (great beef stews here, so I'm told!)? Was it possibly The Little Nibble in Bearwood? Outlaw Studios or was it simply the nearest pub? And where was this 'rundown nightclub on the edge of town'? Hen and Chickens?

On the reverse side was all the lyrics. "Shut your fucking mouth till you know the truth" (later to be edited on a cassette copy by my Dad!). What the fuck did the title 'Thankfully not living in Yorkshire it doesn't apply' mean?

Anyway, Kevin moved from my road in 1981 (around the time of Liars A To E). I continued to follow Dexys for ever more (I was/am the 'Wildhearted Outsider') and in 1995 I set up a Dexys fanzine called 'Keep On Running'. I managed to track down Andy Leek (keyboards on Geno) and through Andy I managed to get in touch with Rowland again. After a few telephone conversations Rowland invited me down for a weekend in Brighton during the summer of 1998, and after some seventeen years he remembered me as a - "serious looking kid"!

Through 'Keep On Running' and the subsequent Dexys tour of 2003 and the latest 'One Day I'm Going To Soar' tour, I've been privileged to meet many great people and many new friends and soul brothers. I am NOT the only wild-hearted outsider.

stuart deabill

Dexys Midnight Runners. The name itself conjures up all kinds of images; a gang on the hop (they were), a team on the blag at speed (can't confirm but possible), a bunch of desperados searching for the young soul rebels (Ok, I'll leave it there).

The band came into my life courtesy of an older lad/mentalist called Richard Bennett, who told everyone that Two Tone was passé and Oddball Records were the new daddy's. How things moved back in '79 and that this record by Dexys was about to be top ten (I'm Just Looking/Dance Stance reached 41 or summit).

By the time Geno was released in April 1980, Two Tone was at its peak, Mod revival and Skinheads were taking over the towns and cities of the UK and the Smelly Heavy Metal was going some as well. Somehow Geno didn't fire my belly up as much as it should have or it does now. Why? God knows, too commercial? How I came to that conclusion is beyond reason – I was 13 for fuck's sake. Anyway, they got to number 1, Kevin didn't look happy about it (similar to Weller in so many ways but never really spoken in the same breath - who knows how they view each other) but The Lambrettas did, so no accounting for smiles/taste on the box.

It was the follow up single There There My Dear that took my head off. The words, written in letter form on the back sleeve as it was sung, were studied for weeks as my still forming outlook, brain matter and depth of knowledge tried to understand what it was about. But like all great 7 inch singles of the day, it enthralled, enticed and smacked home hard how much gravitas this band and song contained. And how Robin was the enemy.

It was only after thinking about how I air tromboned round the bedroom back then, that I now realise that I became a Soul Rebel of sorts and it did ultimately put me in the pure and unadulterated belief that this band could do no wrong ever again. (They didn't).

Searching For The Young Soul Rebels is a complete work of beauty, passion and intensity. The concept, the sleeve, the story of the making of the EMI album just adds to its legend. The 11 songs alone are the real story. They Shall Not Pass.

david corke

I was a manager and promoter and worked with bands like Judas Priest, the Sex Pistols and the Clash. It was part of the second generation of punk that Kevin (Rowland) was doing with a group called the Killjoys. I managed them and then Kevin said he wanted to expand the line-up and do a soul thing. He was responsible for the look that he took from the film On the Waterfront. That's where the idea of the docker look with the sports bag came from.

We did some work with Bernie Rhodes and Dance Stance was put out on Oddball Records. I had a strong relationship with Bernie because I had worked with the Clash for five years as their promoter.

I had an office in Birmingham and was involved in kinds of stuff at the time. I think I had seen the Killjoys at a club in Birmingham that featured a lot of punk stuff. After that Kevin came up to my office and we took it from there. The Killjoys thing was only short lived and then it all changed. Kevin was pretty sharp and he could see how things were moving. I think he saw that punk was gone and he wasn't going to hang around.

1976 was just great. Punk was dangerous, cracking and refreshing. It was so 'rock and roll' and it did away with those pub rock bands. I mean the Pistols came along and just annihilated all of them. I think by the time Kevin had the Killjoys punk already had its masters. Any movement (and the last movement was probably Brit Pop that included bands like Ocean Colour Scene) has a top table and once the top places are taken there's a problem for the developing bands. And there's always a fashion before the music. When Oasis came along every other kid thought they could wear a shirt and a pair of Levis and strut around the street threatening people. It's exciting. Before Oasis came along everything was dead in the water and they came along with a good album.

So I think Kevin saw that punk was gone and he demanded something else. Kevin always had an intensity and they (Dexys) were bound to take off and explode. And then fade… it was never going to last.

Once the Killjoys were gone and Kevin had got rid of everybody, the new band started. The band had a residency in Birmingham that lasted for about six or seven shows. At first they played to friends and about twenty more people and then it developed from there. This was the period of the Dexys personnel that included Geoff, Big Jimmy and Steve Spooner and between them they had a great sound.

In my estimation Kevin Rowland was never a great singer but his delivery was immense and you can say the same for John Lydon and Liam Gallagher. They can't sing but their delivery and intensity can't be denied, and Kevin is well up there along with the likes of Joe Strummer and the others. The other part was the brass which was really full on, it was like the attack of that group. The brass was unrelenting and you couldn't escape it.

I started promoting some stuff at the Cedar Club in Constitution Hill and I convinced the owner to put Dexys on. The venue was packed and the night was an absolute riot. The atmosphere was pretty much verging on punk. You could feel it in the air. I think a lot of that stemmed from Kevin's approach to the audience. Kevin could be very stark and very direct. If he saw someone staring at him in the audience he would challenge them, 'what the fuck are you looking at' and that kind of stuff. And he would couple this with a sort of white Otis Redding awkward stage movement. It was amazing and threatening at the same time. Those Cedar Club shows were the highlights for me and I just knew that they were going to completely take off. I just knew it was going to work. It was slightly on but I remember the Two Tone movement at the time. Dexys, or especially Kevin (Rowland), never wanted to have anything to do with any of that or those bands. But I told the band that we should do the (December '79) tour with The Specials and Madness. They did but Dexys had a completely different feel. But overall I think the tour went down well and also EMI thought it was a good idea.

Kevin wouldn't have anything to do with the other bands and he didn't want them to have anything to do with Dexys. Kevin wanted to keep Dexys very insular and very individual. Trying to keep up with Kevin's intensity was very difficult and I knew then that the band wouldn't be able to keep up and that it wasn't going to last. With Kevin you had be on your toes all the time. At that time he was also very anti people smoking dope. But some of the group loved smoking dope so there were all kinds of attempts to try and hide the fact. I remember being on a boat coming back from the Hook of Holland. A big lump of dope had been purchased and we had to lay wet towels under the bedroom door to stop the fumes from going anywhere in case Kevin found out and got hysterical.

From my point of view Dexys were original, they were tremendous and they became very respected by bands like the Happy Mondays and those Manchester bands.

Kevin was always very edgy with the audiences and would never back down. There was one gig with a load of Cardiff City supporters and it was very much us and them. Kevin and the band always stood their ground. These situations happened in loads of places. Another thing was that Kevin would always insist on playing at strange venues. We went to towns that nobody else had ever been to. I used to have to go on a recon to find these venues and would be asking people in the shops, "Excuse me have you got any town halls, I'm looking for a place to hire?" and the local vicar would say, "Yes of course, as long as there's no swearing". So the band ended up playing to local people and farmers who thought they were going to a dance!

Kevin just liked the idea of playing in venues that no one else had thought about playing. He liked to be different. At that time managing Kevin was nearly impossible. The reason that I left was that I had had enough. I was asked to leave by Kevin but I had sold the contract to Paul Burton. I went to live in Florida. When I did come back I saw Kevin in Broad Street and he said, "So who paid for that" and I said "Well you did because I didn't get any commission from you for about two years".

I had also moved onto the New Romantic scene and was involved with fashion and bands like Duran Duran, and I was the promoter for Spandau Ballet. It had also got to the point where Kevin was making demands on me. I had no time for anything. I wouldn't even have time to have beans on toast. I was on call to Kevin twenty four hours a day, seven days a week because I was his manager. But I tell you what, I wouldn't have changed anything and I would never say anything bad about Dexys. Then, of course, after Dexys imploded I went on to manage the Bureau.

ian jennings

I think I bought Searching For the Young Soul Rebels around my fifteenth birthday. It was an impressionable age. It's an age when you're thinking of your career choices, doing your exams and then, from out of nowhere, this music appears. I vividly remember Dance Stance because I was asked to write a review on a play, book or film for some homework. So I reviewed an episode of Top of the Pops. It was Dexys first TOTP's performance. The thing was Dance Stance had done nothing for me but the Specials had Too Much Too Young and Madness had My Girl. I thought these songs were a lot more fun. So Dance Stance sort of passed me by and then Geno came out. At the time I was attending my local youth club and northern soul was a massive thing. Where I lived in North Yorkshire it was huge and I would see the buses going to the Wigan Casino (but I was too young to go). I was watching these older people dance to these northern soul sounds and then Geno came along with the B-side, Breaking Down the Walls of Heartache, which was a northern soul song. And it got me thinking 'who are this band? What's this Geno all about?'.

From here I revisited Dance Stance, then there was the single There There My Dear and then the album. When the album came out it was just so unique. You just couldn't compare it to anything else. It was like a bunch of some very angry kids playing some northern soul music… but with a punk edge. I remember Steve Spooner once said to me "We were a punk band playing soul music".

At the time Dexys were a band playing soul when other bands were playing ska, punk and new wave. But Dexys stood out and I remember, even today, the day when Geno came out and who I was with. It made that much of an impression on me. I was with a friend and two girls (that we were trying to get off with) and we were sitting in this little field, in this little hamlet, on the outskirts of Selby (where I lived) with a transistor radio. We were listening to the top 40 count down and when Geno was announced as number one I jumped up and down like I had scored a goal in a big football match. It meant that much to me.

Then there was the image of the gang (Dexys). I mean, I'm fifteen years old and I want to be in a gang and be part of something. So seeing these guys all dressed the same in woolly hats, with all that attitude, I was like that's me, that's what I want to be. I want to carry that bag and walk away into that darkness and find that something that I had been searching for.

I was very lucky because by the time I was eighteen I was also going to the northern soul all-nighters and I was seeing those same older boys that I used to look up to. I remember going to the all-nighters with that Dexys image… that Stokers image with the band. I was leaving my home at eleven at night and driving all over the country trying to find that music. And I'm still trying to find that music and that Searching for the Young Soul Rebels album was the start of all that for me.

That album (Rebels) was a natural progression into soul music. The other thing was it was all very working class - council house, estates types who loved Dexys music in the same way they had northern soul music. That whole black American soul music does come so naturally. I dunno if it's because we're trying to get out from where we are or we're just looking for something else that's different from what's around us. I don't know but that album (Rebels) made me want to go and discover other things. It made me want to go and discover northern soul a bit deeper. I wanted to know more about who wrote Seven Days is Too Long. I wanted to know what else was out there and my love of northern soul developed because of that album.

It wasn't the same for everyone and I remember one fella saying to me that he loved Dexys until they covered a northern soul song. The scene is a very prickly thing. Lots of Northern soul people back then didn't want northern soul in the charts or being popularized. They wanted it kept exclusive.

Whenever I find myself talking about the 'Rebels' album I always find myself talking about northern soul. I mean there's only one northern soul track on the album but you can hear the influences all over it. There was even some talk about Dexys playing at the Wigan Casino. I spoke with Kevin Archer and was convinced that they had played there but I'm not sure they did. It was on the bands schedule at one point. It was listed on one of the tours. I also spoke to Russ Winstanley too and he said they didn't play there.

2010 was the thirtieth anniversary of 'Searching For the Young Soul Rebels' and, being known as a fairly good organiser, some people suggested that I organise something to do with the album. I contacted Geoff (Blythe) who was in New York and asked him when he was next over in the UK and he just happened to be over in the next July. After this I started contacting the others linked to the album. Big Jimmy hadn't played a note for something like sixteen years but said he would try. Then I got Stone Foundation involved, who I had seen support (with an acoustic set) the Bureau in 2005. They rang me and said they had heard I was putting this 'do' on and they wanted to play at it. So I went to see them as their full seven piece outfit and they absolutely blew me away. So they were in and at the 'do' Big Jimmy and JB played live with them. I remember during the sound check that Jimmy looked so nervous, I didn't think he was going to do it, but when he hit that trombone - it was just like wow! There were tears rolling down people's faces - Big Jimmy was back!

Other good things were that Steve Spooner had driven from Cornwall, Mike Laye had flown over from France, Anthony O'Shaugnessy (the guy from the front cover that I tracked down) was there. It was a really good night.

archie brown

Our (the Upset) connection to Dexys came about via an agent and Seb Shelton. Seb became the drummer with Secret Affair but he was also drumming for the Young Bucks, which was my first band. At the time Seb used to wear this slick suit with small lapels and thin black tie and he had a crew cut which was quite strange at the time. I'm talking here about pre-punk and before the Sex Pistols. Somehow Seb already had that image. Then when Secret Affair saw the Young Bucks in London they decided they wanted Seb as their drummer. So he joined them and stayed with them for a couple of years before leaving to come and manage my band. He had some connections from his time with Secret Affair and got us involved with an agent. This agent got us some gigs and they were for the Dexys tour.

What I remember from the tour was some gigs in Wales, when some of the audience were shouting 'Upset, Upset' through the Dexys set. Rowland was furious.

Whilst that tour was going on Geno went to number one. Getting to gigs meant we all had to travel in a van with another band called the Black Arabs. There were five of them and four of us. Dexys travelled in their own mini-bus. We had a roadie guy whose name was Biffo (he went on to do stuff that included the

Bureau) and he also did the driving. The Black Arabs was Bernie Rhodes' band and he was forever taking them off the tour to do other things. So they would disappear but then, when they came back, there would be another guy singing and then they would disappear again and on it went. So much of that tour was done with just us and Dexys.

It was during that tour that I started to get on pretty well with Geoff and Steve. I also played sax, so we would sit around chatting about saxophones and all that stuff. The other thing was that they never had any money. We were the support band but we were getting paid (money per-day), were staying in cheap hotels and had enough to eat. What we did get paid was enough to buy a couple of beers and a packet of fags but basically they (Dexys) weren't getting anything and you would have Geoff saying in his gruff voice, "Have you got any cigarettes?" So we would be giving them fags. The only beer they would get was if there was some kind of rider. And all this was happening while Geno was number one and I was thinking 'Shit, is this what the music business is all about'.

Another thing was some of those gigs on that tour were really empty. I remember we were going to venues all around the coast. It was a brilliant idea but it didn't really work because we were doing these strange places and people didn't come. There was one gig where there was only six people in the audience and once the Upset came off stage there was ten! That tour certainly wasn't all glamour.

We played at the end of a big, long, wooden pier. This meant that the roadies had to haul all the equipment along to the end of this pier, which was right out in the sea. Then while they were doing it this massive fuckin' storm happened. The wooden boards had like an inch of water on them. You couldn't stand up in it. The roadies were slipping all over the place and they were so mad. It was hilarious. Another time we played in some tent and there was all this mud. It was like being at Glastonbury. The roadies just hated it.

On the tour Dexys always seemed to be having meetings. They would go on for hours and I would ask them what they had been talking about and they wouldn't be able to say - it was all top secret!

There was also Keith Allen on that tour. Kevin (Rowland) would say to him "What I want you to do is go out there and slag off the British Army". Now the thing was back then there were a lot of skinhead type people that followed Dexys and so Keith's bit didn't go down well. There wasn't one fuckin' laugh. But Keith has got some balls and he just went on with it but eventually got sick of it and started doing his normal act, which then of course, went down a storm. I also remember five minutes into his act the stage lights went out. This was because Kevin (Rowland) had told the light guy to turn them off. But one of the crew, whose name was Beamer, stood up on the PA and shone a torch on Keith so he could continue. It was brilliant. The audience at the time seemed to attract a lot of people that liked the Two Tone and mod thing. They didn't really attract the punks but there was a real mixture and there would be some trouble. I mean Jerry Dammers hated all that stuff. I had met Jerry years before because he had gone to school with the Young Bucks bass player. In the early days he would come up and play some keyboards with us. This was around 1976 and way before he formed the Specials. So the Specials were attracting the kind of people they were against in some ways and I think Dexys had a similar problem.

So doing those gigs with Dexys meant that I got to know the Searching For the Young Soul Rebels album pretty well. I never actually owned it but I heard it every night whilst we played these strange places around the coastline. We did play some big, well-known venues and they were full.

Rowland liked the Upset because we had this kind of country soul sound and it fitted in with what he was doing. The Upset were signed to London Records and we had two singles put out by them. Then Seb told us that he couldn't manage us anymore because he had been asked by Kevin (Rowland) to join Dexys. It was a real shit for me because it was going great for us. But then I got asked to sing for the Bureau, so I joined up with some of the guys from Dexys (Blythe, Williams, Stoker, Spooner and Talbot). That Dexys band did very well very quickly but then very quickly fell apart.

geoff blythe dexys demise of the young soul rebels

I just knew it was all over when, during a rehearsal somewhere in the arse-end of Birmingham (I forget where), Rowland took me aside and told me that I should learn to play the fiddle and likewise, Jim, the cello.

Hello, we're a soul band. What the…?

The beginning of the end. I had believed in the Soul Rebels kudos, as did most of us. It was not a gimmick but a commitment to an organic approach that, we believed, was destined to produce more classic work in the future. Apparently, however, Rowland had decided that it had run its course and, therefore, he needed to re-invent himself. Even he could contain the Soul Rebels no longer.

That was it… Requiem Aeternam. A wonderful spell was cast that still enthrals today and no such is cast without much pain, and much joy. It has inspired many and all but destroyed some.

It lives on, and I suppose, at the end of the day, that is all that one can ask.

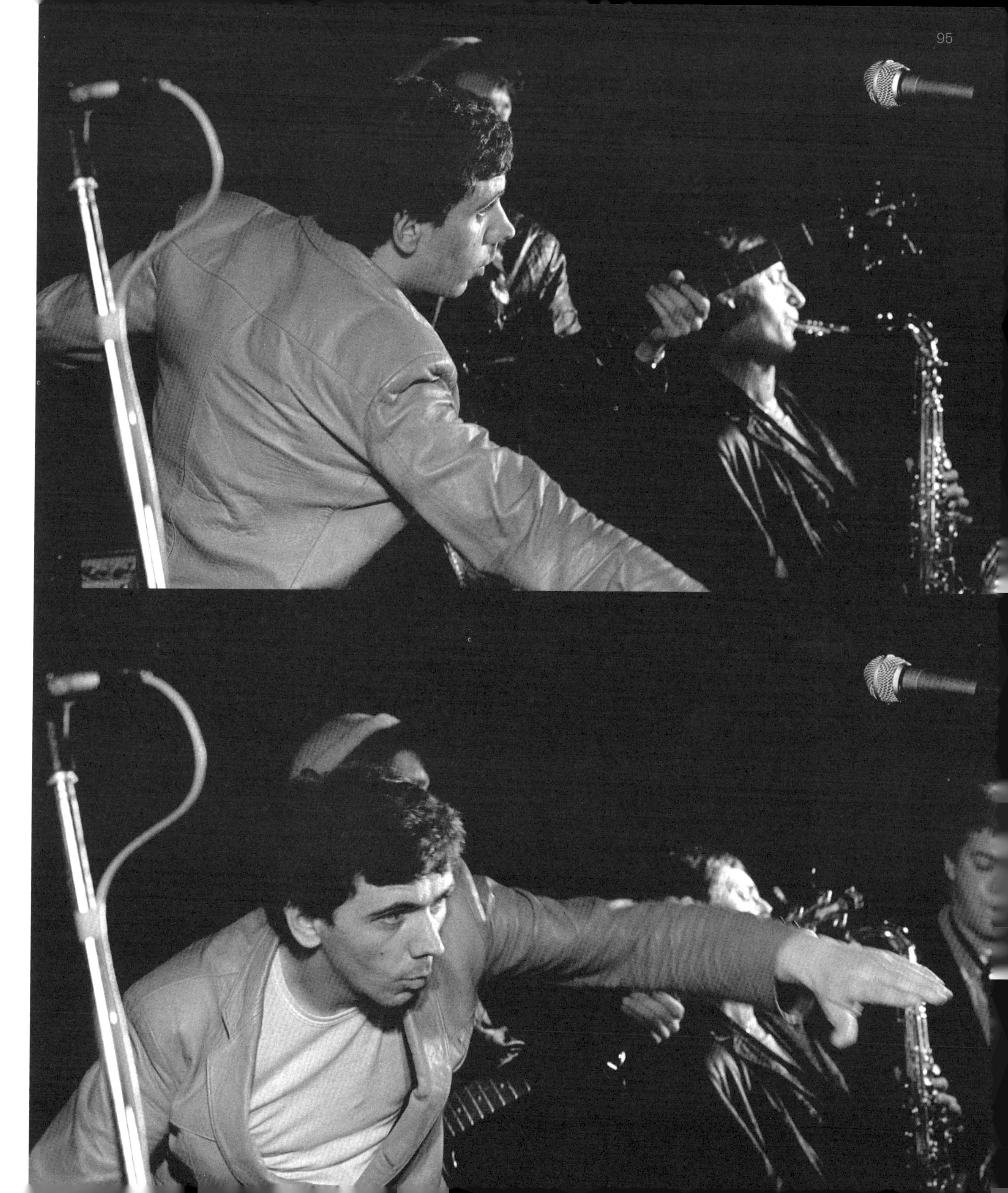

BF

14

14

TAXIS
ONLY

PRICE

ALL UNDER

THANKS AND DEDICATIONS

Special thanks from Geoff Blythe to the following: My wife Clare for all her support, in this and all my endeavors. My daughters, Charlotte and Alice. Friends and fellow soul rebels Steve Spooner, Big Jim Paterson, Kev Archer and Pete Williams for their understanding, and sometimes jogging my memory. And finally Lamb and Pete Lamont for aiding and abetting.

Mike Laye would like to thank Mark Hodgson at Hand for doing such a wonderful job with the layout, Ian and Mark for getting the project off the ground in the first place and Countdown for making it a reality at the end. Oh… and, of course, the boys in the band!

Snowy would like to thank Geoff and Mike and Pete for doing the book with him. Ian Jennings and all the contributors, Donna, Ian, Mark and Paul at Countdown Books. And he dedicates this book to his daughter Josie '7 days too long', Loz for putting up with another book and his old pal Paul Crittenden for nicking my copy of rebels from Woolies in the first place way back in 1980!

Pete McKenna would like to thank all the Countdown team for making this happen. To Snowy, to Mister Geoff Blythe for his evocative words, to the KSC lads Matty Morris, Paul Crittenden and Ray Waller for the barrel of laughs we shared at Margate. To Ged Grennell and family, to George Dorling and Warren Schofield always. It just wouldn't be the same without you. Keep On Keeping On.

Countdown Publishing would like to thank Donna Boardman for proof reading. Mark, Kerri and Archie at Hand. Cess and Danny at the Gladstone, The legend that is Spizz, The legend that is Vicki Hallam and all who went to the Outrigger in Brum back in the mid 80s. Kirsty Walker, Anna Picton and Krystle Coe, Maddy and Hollie, Lucie Coe, Charlie Jefferies, all at Merc, our friends at Sherrys. Remembering Ilan Ostrove and Simon Bullock.